Maybe Lynn Didn't Think Marriage Was A Good Idea, But Russ Knew It Was The Only Answer. He Didn't Give His Word Lightly.

Lynn's brother had looked him directly in the eyes and asked if Russ was going to marry Lynn. Unable to lie about the situation, Russ had gone along with Lynn's ruse, knowing in his heart that he'd meant it.

He knew he was in dangerous territory. He'd made up his mind a long time ago not to get emotionally involved with another woman, and until he'd ended up in bed with Lynn McCall, he'd had no trouble sticking to his plans to remain single and detached.

Despite what had happened between him and Lynn, he wasn't going to allow her to get close enough to hurt him. He wasn't going to put his heart on the line. Besides, he knew it wouldn't be a forever-after kind of relationship. It wouldn't even be a real marriage.

Of course, if she was pregnant with his child, that would change the stakes quite a bit....

11684158

Dear Reader,

Welcome to Silhouette Desire, where you can spice up your April with six passionate, powerful and provocative romances!

Beloved author Diana Palmer delivers a great read with *A Man of Means,* the latest in her LONG, TALL TEXANS miniseries, as a saucy cook tames a hot-tempered cowboy with her biscuits. Then, enjoy reading how one woman's orderly life is turned upside down when she is wooed by *Mr. Temptation,* April's MAN OF THE MONTH and the first title in Cait London's hot new HEARTBREAKERS miniseries.

Reader favorite Maureen Child proves a naval hero is no match for a determined single mom in *The SEAL's Surrender,* the latest DYNASTIES: THE CONNELLYS title. And a reluctant widow gets a second chance at love in *Her Texan Tycoon* by Jan Hudson.

The drama continues in the TEXAS CATTLEMAN'S CLUB: THE LAST BACHELOR continuity series with *Tall, Dark...and Framed?* by Cathleen Galitz, when an attractive defense attorney falls head over heels for her client— a devastatingly handsome tycoon with a secret. And discover what a ranch foreman, a virgin and her protective brothers have in common in *One Wedding Night...* by Shirley Rogers.

Celebrate the season by pampering yourself with all six of these exciting new love stories.

Enjoy!

Joan Marlow Golan

Joan Marlow Golan
Senior Editor, Silhouette Desire

Please address questions and book requests to:
Silhouette Reader Service
U.S.: 3010 Walden Ave., P.O. Box 1325, Buffalo, NY 14269
Canadian: P.O. Box 609, Fort Erie, Ont. L2A 5X3

One Wedding Night...
SHIRLEY ROGERS

Silhouette®

Desire

Published by Silhouette Books

America's Publisher of Contemporary Romance

If you purchased this book without a cover you should be aware that this book is stolen property. It was reported as "unsold and destroyed" to the publisher, and neither the author nor the publisher has received any payment for this "stripped book."

 SILHOUETTE BOOKS

ISBN 0-373-76434-0

ONE WEDDING NIGHT...

Copyright © 2002 by Shirley Rogerson Inc.

All rights reserved. Except for use in any review, the reproduction or utilization of this work in whole or in part in any form by any electronic, mechanical or other means, now known or hereafter invented, including xerography, photocopying and recording, or in any information storage or retrieval system, is forbidden without the written permission of the editorial office, Silhouette Books, 300 East 42nd Street, New York, NY 10017 U.S.A.

All characters in this book have no existence outside the imagination of the author and have no relation whatsoever to anyone bearing the same name or names. They are not even distantly inspired by any individual known or unknown to the author, and all incidents are pure invention.

This edition published by arrangement with Harlequin Books S.A.

® and TM are trademarks of Harlequin Books S.A., used under license. Trademarks indicated with ® are registered in the United States Patent and Trademark Office, the Canadian Trade Marks Office and in other countries.

Visit Silhouette at www.eHarlequin.com

Printed in U.S.A.

Books by Shirley Rogers

Silhouette Desire

Cowboys, Babies and Shotgun Vows #1176
Conveniently His #1266
A Cowboy, a Bride & a Wedding Vow #1344
Baby of Fortune #1384
One Wedding Night... #1434

SHIRLEY ROGERS

lives in Virginia with her husband, two cats and an adorable Maltese named Blanca. She has two grown children, a son and a daughter. As a child, she was known for having a vivid imagination. It wasn't until she started reading romances that she realized her true destiny was writing them! Besides reading, she enjoys traveling, seeing movies and spending time with her family.

To Diana, my wonderful brainstorming partner,
with deep appreciation. And to my terrific editor,
Tina Colombo.

One

Russ Logan rolled onto his side in his double bed and felt something warm and exquisitely soft beneath his palm.

A woman's body.

Still deep in the dregs of sleep, he savored the enticing fragments of the erotic dream, sliding his hand over smooth skin and letting it rest on a soft round mound. A very real erotic dream, his subconscious told him. He let his imagination run with it, feeling his own body's quickening response.

Without warning, pain slammed through his brain, distorting the dream and the illusion of a blond-haired, blue-eyed angel. Russ struggled through the depths of the dream to the edge of reality and very slowly pried open one eye.

He was in his own room. Sunshine shone brightly through a gap in familiar dusky brown curtains.

Thank God. Closing his eyes, he knew a moment of relief. Drawing a ragged breath, he struggled to get his bearings. His mind swam, and his stomach felt like lead heated to the boiling point. Finally, forcing both eyes open, he stared straight into the lovely face of Lynn McCall.

Hell.

Jerking his hand away from her breast, Russ shot up into a sitting position. His sudden movements caused her to stir, and her eyelids lifted, slowly at first, then widening as they began to focus on him. He watched the realization of where she was dawn on her just before her harsh, ear-piercing scream echoed throughout the room and his already pounding head. Russ was sure it was heard as far away from the west Texas ranch as San Antonio. He put his hand to the ear closest to Lynn and covered it.

"Stop that!" he barked, cutting his eyes at her, his mind just beginning to catalog a hangover and the pulverizing headache that came with it.

"Don't come near me!" Lynn scrambled up against the backboard of his bed, dragging the sheet up and over her, clutching it tightly, covering what she could of herself and just about yanking it totally off of him.

Russ grabbed at it just before it exposed all the gifts God gave him. "If you scream like that again, believe me, that won't be a hardship," he grated, his teeth clenched against the throbbing in his head. He was sure a blood vessel was about to explode.

She stared at him as if he had two heads. Red blotches stained her cheeks. "What...what are you doing here?" she demanded, gasping for air.

He eyed her cautiously, his expression guarded as

he fought to keep his eyes open. The ability to breathe was suddenly as difficult as believing this was really happening. The girl who worked beside him every day in worn jeans and dirty boots didn't exist. In her place was a beautiful young woman.

Naked! In your bed!

Her tousled blond hair was cropped short and framed her heart-shaped face. Bare of makeup, her flawless skin glowed. His gaze slid lower, past the gentle slope of her neckline, pausing for a moment on her full breasts hidden beneath the white sheet. Russ's gaze lingered there long enough to wonder how it would feel to have his mouth on them, then he wisely diverted his attention to her face. "I think a more appropriate question is, 'What are *you* doing in *my* bed?'" He leaned forward and held his head in his hands, moaning in agony.

Damn. What on earth had happened last night? he wondered, trying to make some sense of the incredible dream turned nightmare. Sleeping with his boss's sister! He must have lost his mind—and most certainly he'd lost his job along with it.

Russ thought about the previous evening. Flashbacks tormented him. He really couldn't remember drinking too much at Lynn's brother's wedding reception, only a few beers. Of course, everyone had toasted Jake and Catherine several times. A lot of partying had gone on long after the bride and groom had left. Damn! When was the last time he'd drunk enough to lose control of his senses?

However, it didn't take much alcohol to dull someone's senses—or to take advantage of another person's loss of inhibitions. And he had to wonder how much he'd wanted Lynn to let this happen. Had he subconsciously just ignored his inner warnings that she was forbidden?

"Your bed?" Lynn wailed, squinting. She closed her eyes, then very slowly reopened them, hoping that this was some horrible dream. Looking around the large room, her gaze swept past a dresser and a small refrigerator, coming to rest on a television positioned on the wall opposite the foot of the bed. Though she'd never been in the foreman's quarters, she began to recognize the room as one of the buildings on the McCall ranch. "Oh, no! Oh, please tell me this isn't really happening."

Pain came crashing down on her, and she put a hand to her forehead. What *had* happened last night? She tried to remember, but it hurt to think. It hurt just to breathe. She felt like she was going to die, and heaven knows, she deserved to. The contents of her stomach rolled. Unable to face Russ, she kept her head turned away.

Russ Logan! She was in bed, *naked,* with Russ Logan. Oh, jeez, she'd done some stupid things in her life, but never anything *this* stupid. Her mind swam with possible solutions of getting herself out of this with at least a touch of dignity.

Russ watched her facial expression change from shock to disbelief to humiliation. She pulled her legs up and tucked her forehead on her knees. Her blond bangs fell forward and covered her rose-colored nails. Damn, she was sexy as hell, he thought, running his gaze over her bare shoulders and arms, then down to the sheet covering the rest of her. She moaned again, and he hauled his mind back to the problem facing him.

"Take it easy," Russ coaxed, and he instinctively

reached toward her. As if sensing he was going to touch her, she gripped the sheet even tighter as her head whipped around.

"Don't you dare touch me!" she snapped, then groaned, her gaze focused just over his right shoulder. Panic seized every muscle in her face, twisting her lovely features in contortions he wouldn't have thought possible.

Despite his own anguish, Russ slowly shook his head. He gave a slight chuckle that sounded more sarcastic than humorous. "I think it's a little late for you to be saying that," he stated flatly, realizing that a whole lot more than touching had gone on during the night. An image of her soft and pliant beneath him, of him slowly sliding into her, played like a detailed erotic movie in his mind. "And, dammit, don't raise your voice again." Despite his cursing, it came out sounding like a plea.

"I'm sorry," Lynn murmured, a trace of fear and humiliation still in her eyes. She looked at him and winced, then just as quickly turned her head away as tears gathered in the corners of her eyes. She was going to die of embarrassment. That, or by the hands of her three older brothers, whichever came first. She swallowed hard and managed to calm herself enough to speak rationally. "Would you please just get out of the bed and hand me my clothes?"

He started to throw the sheet back, and she screamed again, stilling his movements. He shot her a warning stare, looking as if he wanted to strangle her.

"No! Wait! Just stay where you are!" she demanded, realizing he was as naked as she was. "And...oh...please, please, don't move again. My

stomach feels like it's on the ocean." The temptation
to throw up all over everything was inching closer to
reality.

Russ swore under his breath, but he was grateful
that she'd relented. His entire body ached. "Don't
worry. I don't think I can move anyway."

They moaned in unison, then he raised his head.
He opened his mouth to speak, but was suddenly at
a loss for words. He stared at her, silenced by her
beauty and by the fact that he'd spent the night making love to her. As if aware of his scrutiny, she looked
at him, and their eyes finally connected. It seemed
she was as shocked as he was to find herself in his
bed.

She had the McCall blue eyes, a trait she shared
with two of her brothers. Only on Lynn, those blue
eyes could bring a man to his knees. When she
smiled, well, Russ figured there wasn't a man for
miles who wouldn't want to have her smiling at him.

But he wasn't the right man for her, and he damn
well knew it—as well as he knew making love with
her last night had been a huge mistake. Besides the
fact that she was a McCall and hands-off, she was
too innocent, too sweet, too trusting. And he was too
cynical, too jaded.

And too damn old. At thirty, he was ten years older
and wiser. He'd tried marriage once, and it had ended
in disaster. He wouldn't be making that mistake
again.

"Look," Russ began, speaking softly so that his
head wouldn't detonate, "I'm not proud about admitting it, but I'm not exactly sure how this happened.
What do you remember?" He hoped she had a better

idea than him. Maybe something she said would trigger his own mind, trick it into remembering.

Staring at him as if he was an apparition, Lynn felt like she was in a hypnotic trance. Everything that had happened last night, *everything,* was slowly coming back to her, but there was no way she was going to confess what she remembered. Her eyes lost their glaze, and her gaze slowly slipped over Russ's wide shoulders and well-muscled arms to the pattern of dark hair on his chest. Her heartbeat quickened. *She'd kissed him there!*

She mentally jerked herself back from going there and tried to focus on what had happened the night before. *Jake's reception.* Lynn had a vague memory of having fun at the reception, drinking a little and flirting a lot. With Russ. And dancing with him. Many times. Slow, seductive dances where he'd held her in his arms and his body had moved in rhythm against hers, stirring up all kinds of wants and needs she hadn't been conscious of before.

Russ! The one person in the world she thought was a chauvinistic, overbearing, insufferable… She stopped her inner ranting as it began to worsen her headache. Sure, Russ was handsome, ruggedly so, with dark brown hair and deep, sea-green eyes that rarely revealed his innermost feelings.

He'd come to the ranch asking for a job one day and had talked at length with Jake. Her brother had hired Russ on a trial basis. After a short while, he'd made a name for himself throughout the area. Word had quickly spread from Crockett to Ozona and San Luis about his incredible skill with horses, and in addition to training the Bar M's quarter horses, he trained horses for other ranchers.

She'd started working with him over a year ago, but they were barely able to tolerate one another. Well, they'd done a lot more than tolerate each other last night, she thought, shrinking a little more away from him.

"Lynn?"

His voice drew her attention back to him, and she felt her cheeks flame. "What?"

Russ frowned, drawing his dark brown eyebrows into a vee. "Can you help me out here a little?"

She shook her head, then cringed when pain slammed her again. "Not really," she told him, fully aware of the images of Russ kissing her appearing in her mind. "I don't remember all that much, either," she fibbed.

Russ sank back down onto the bed, straightening his body and crossing his forearm over his face.

"What are you doing?" she demanded, glaring at him.

"Trying to keep my head from firing off like a rocket," he answered, cracking open an eye, then closing it again.

The night before began coming back in very slow sketches. Drinking a little, dancing with Lynn. Kissing her. *Wanting her.*

Bringing her back to his room.

Making love to her—hot, achingly lustful love to her. Several times.

She was a virgin!

Russ felt as if his entire world had shifted, and he was about to slide into a void of darkness. He'd taken her virginity!

You really screwed up. Big time. Not only had he hurt Lynn, he'd hurt her entire family.

Her brothers were going to kill him. And rightly so. He'd do the same thing if someone had taken advantage of his sister. Not that he had one. But he could understand their desire to protect Lynn.

The silence in the room closed in on him. He forced his eyes open and looked at her, then stopped himself from blurting an empty apology. Hell, an apology of any kind wasn't exactly appropriate. Unfortunately, it was all he could offer.

"Lynn, I'm sorry," he said, his voice husky with regret. He rolled onto his side, and his gaze met hers squarely. "This should never have happened. I take full responsibility."

"What?" Lynn's eyes widened, and her blond brows rose.

"I should never have brought you here. I should have been in control enough to stop myself from touching you."

"Well, thank you very much," she snapped, wishing she could crawl into a hole and disappear. "It's just wonderful for a woman to hear how much a man didn't really want to be with her the morning *after* she made love with him." Her voice cracked, and she damned herself for it.

"Hell, honey, I didn't mean it like that," he said, trying again to apologize, but feeling as if he was digging a deeper hole for himself. Moving slowly, he sat up. "I don't want to hurt your feelings, I swear." He started to touch her, and she stiffened. Letting his hand drop, he studied her. Her hurt expression tore at his insides. He wasn't getting this right at all. Hell, he was out of practice. It had been a long time since he'd had a morning after.

"Don't worry, I don't expect you to make an honest woman of me," she retorted.

Russ welcomed the relief that washed over him, then just as quickly admonished himself. He should have been thinking of doing exactly that. When her brothers found out about this, there'd be hell to pay. Not only that, but if anyone saw him and Lynn come in here, her reputation was ruined.

And he'd taken her virginity.

Hell and damnation. Annoyed with himself and the world as a whole, he stared into her blue eyes. Confusion and hurt lingered in them, mixed with disappointment and a trace of fear.

He smiled crookedly, and his gaze sought hers. "Well, if it'll make you feel any better, I'll tell you what I do remember about last night." She didn't say anything, just clamped her beautifully sculpted lips together. Russ forged on, "I have an incredible memory of holding you and kissing you." The flush that had barely disappeared from her face returned in a rush. "I remember how sweet and giving you were when I took you the first time, and how thoroughly sexy you were the second and third."

Tears appeared in her eyes, and a hard knot tightened in his gut. "Honey, please don't cry," he pleaded, feeling at a loss. He was trying to make her feel better, not worse.

Staring at him with pure dismay, Lynn swiped at her wet cheeks. "Believe me, I don't want to." Realizing that she'd given her virginity to Russ, she was at a loss for words. She'd given him firsthand, *personal* proof of her innocence.

Well, she thought dejectedly, she couldn't say she was inexperienced anymore, could she? Of all the men for her to sleep with! Visions of them making love assailed her, and she closed her eyes as she relived the memory of being with him. Her recollection was foggy at best, but she knew he'd been tender and gentle, and she was just as sure she hadn't asked him to stop. In fact, begging and pleading came to her mind.

What did that say about her judgment? She and Russ didn't even get along most of the time. He'd been trying to get rid of her since Jake had finally agreed to let her work with the horses on the Bar M.

"Look, this is just as much my fault as yours," she stated, grimacing at him and still looking offended.

Russ's expression turned grim. "Don't say that. This is my fault, not yours. You're the innocent party here. I'm sure I don't have to remind you *how* innocent," he grated, still angry at himself. "I'm a hell of a lot more experienced than you are. I should have shown some control. I—"

A nervous chuckle came from her throat, and she shook her head. "That kind of macho thinking is ridiculous."

"Well, it might well seem ridiculous, but it's the damned truth," he stated, his tone gruff. "Now I guess the best thing for us to do is to figure out what to do about this."

Her mouth fell open. "What do you mean?" His biceps bulged as he crossed his arms over his chest, and Lynn had to suppress the urge to touch him. A flutter of excitement coiled through her as she remembered being held in those strong arms.

He sat up straighter and leaned against the headboard, stretching his legs out in front of him. "In case you haven't figured it out, we've gotten ourselves in a situation here.''

A *situation*. Well, if Lynn had a niggling curiosity as to how Russ was analyzing what had happened between them, it was erased by his terming it a "situation." Her temper beginning to simmer, she gave him a scorching look. "If you'll just turn your back, I'll get my clothes on and get out of here and there won't be a *situation* to worry about."

Russ wasn't sure why, but knowing she wanted to hightail it out of his bed stuck in his craw. She looked so absolutely desirable that he wanted to drag her against him and kiss her luscious mouth. Curbing his desire, he said, "You think it's gonna be that easy, huh?"

Lynn wasn't sure how to react to his question. "What are you getting at?"

"Well, for one thing, honey, we work side by side every single day. I don't know about you, but I'm sure as hell not gonna be able to look at you the way I used to."

Lynn's expression turned indignant. "And exactly how was that?" she demanded, tucking the sheet under her arms to free her hands. Russ slid his gaze lazily over her, and she felt as if he'd somehow touched her.

"You were hands-off, honey. I'm not fool enough to think that I'm in the same league as you. In my right mind, I would never have laid a hand on you," he admitted. Now, thanks to his lack of control and poor judgment, he was going to have to work with her remembering how damn fantastic it felt being with her.

Not sure of what to think, Lynn was quiet for a

moment. She had known Russ for almost five years. He'd started working at the Bar M when she was sixteen. He'd never said much to her, and she'd always thought he just didn't like her. It surprised her to learn that he thought himself beneath her.

She thought about how very little she knew about him. He'd come from somewhere in Montana, but she didn't think he had a family, mainly because to her knowledge he'd never had anyone call for him or come to see him. She'd always thought that kind of sad. Her family had often included Russ in celebrations at the ranch, but frequently he was the first to leave, seeming to prefer his own company.

Russ shook his head. "And then there's our age difference. I'm a hell of a lot older than you." Before she could say anything, he held up his hand to stop her. "Not only that, but you're the boss's little sister."

Affronted, Lynn glared at him. He sure had a lot of excuses for *not* wanting her! "Well, let me give you a few more minutes so you can just keep adding up why this was such a horrible mistake. It's not as if I *planned* it, you know."

"Hell, Lynn, I'm saying this all wrong. I'm not good enough for you. You're beautiful and intelligent." He said it as if it killed him to admit it, but, hell, it was the truth, now that he'd seen her as a woman. "Any man would be lucky to marry you."

Except him, of course. He wouldn't be giving his heart to another woman. No way, not in *this* lifetime. One go-round with Candace had taught him a bitter lesson. When he'd found out she was pregnant with another man's baby, he'd walked out and never looked back.

"Jeez, thanks so much."

"And besides the fact that I'm too old for you, Jake'll have my hide when he gets back from his honeymoon, if Ryder and Deke leave any for him."

"What my brothers think isn't important," Lynn insisted, forgetting her hurt feelings for the moment.

"Well, if you believe that, you're more innocent than I thought. The way I see it, I'll be off this ranch by sundown."

She made a snorting sound. "Don't be ridiculous, Russ. You're not going to get fired because you slept with me."

His lip curled. "Hell, Lynn, the only reason I'm still here is because no one knows you're in my bed. Mark my words, I'll be gone in a matter of hours."

Would he? Lynn wondered. Were her brothers *that* protective? Well, they *had* threatened every boy she'd dated with bodily harm if he laid a hand on her. And the single hands on the ranch *did* give her a wide berth when she was around them.

Was Russ right? She didn't especially like him— which sounded ridiculous because she'd just spent the night making love with him—but she sure didn't want to be the cause of him losing his job. "No one knows I'm, uh, we're here together. All I have to do is get dressed and get up to the house. No one will ever find out we spent the night together."

"*I'll* know," Russ declared irritably. "And if we get caught, the entire town of Crockett will know."

Lynn wasn't paying attention. She'd begun to look around the room, searching for the time. There was a small, round alarm clock on his dresser.

"Nine o'clock!" she screamed. Frantic, she waved at him with her hands. "Just turn around, and I'll get dressed and get out of here! Quick!'' She was going to have to try and sneak into the house. By now, Ryder, his wife Ashley and their babies would be up. Maybe, if the Fates were with Lynn, she could get in the front door and down the hall to her room before she came upon them.

''What are you gonna do? Sneak in?'' Russ asked, sounding as if that would never work in a million years.

Lynn made a face at him. ''Yes, I'm going to sneak in. If I hurry, I can make it.'' She wished she had some regular clothes here, but, of course, she didn't. ''Turn around!'' she commanded, searching for the beautiful blue dress she'd worn at the wedding. It was lying on the floor out of her reach, as were her skimpy lace panties. Heat surged to her face all over again.

Russ stared at her as if she'd lost her mind, then he shrugged his shoulders. He started to move, then stopped when they both heard a loud knock at the door. Panic swept through Lynn as both of their heads whipped in that direction. Her chest got heavy as she and Russ looked back at each other. A feeling of dread hung over her and she held her breath. Russ put his finger to his lips, motioning for her to keep quiet.

The knock came again, louder and more demanding. Russ jumped out of bed and grabbed his jeans, pulling them on and zipping them just as he heard Ryder call his name.

Then the door flew open.

Two

"Sorry for barging in, Russ," Ryder McCall blurted, bursting into the room, his boot heels thundering on the hardwood floor.

"What's going on?" Russ stepped forward, blocking his path, hoping to also block Ryder's view of Lynn at the same time. Having had just enough time to zip his pants, but not enough to close the snap, he let his hands linger there.

"We can't find Lynn anywhere." Ryder's face was set into a permanent frown as he whipped his hat off and hit it against his thigh. His voice sounded deeply troubled. "She didn't come home last night, and Ashley's really worried about her. Lynn doesn't do things like this. She's—" The words died a natural death when a movement from the bed caught his eye.

"Damn, I'm sorry, man, I shouldn't have come busting in here unannounced." He started to turn away, then caught sight of a familiar blue dress on the floor near the foot of the bed. He frowned, then turned back toward Russ. He didn't say anything in the split second it took to make the connection, then his gaze went beyond Russ and landed hard on his sister, who was sitting in the rumpled bed with the sheet clutched to her neck.

"What in hell is going on here?" Ryder demanded, his gaze taking in the intimate scene in bits and pieces—Russ barely dressed, clothes strewn here and there. His sister naked! Anger glittered in his eyes. "Why, you—"

He rounded on Russ, his fist flying. Russ backed up and ducked, but not quite quick enough to avoid Ryder's punch. The powerful blow to Russ's chin knocked him backward, and he stumbled. He quickly regained his footing, then faced Ryder, his stance rigid. Bracing himself for another blow, he brought his arms up to protect himself.

"Ryder!" Lynn screamed, "stop it!" She barely got the words out as her brother charged toward Russ. "Stop!" Her shrill voice echoed through the room.

Russ deflected the next punch with his forearm, then shoved Ryder away with enough force to give him time to regain his own bearing. "Hold on, Ryder!" he growled, raising his hands, palms out.

Lynn screamed again, stopping Ryder in his tracks, his fists raised. Fierce protectiveness raged in his eyes. Both men were breathing rapidly, both glaring at each other with malicious intent. Ryder's eyes were fraught with suspicion. "Who the hell do you think you are?" he demanded.

"Look, just give me a chance to explain," Russ said in a rush. He rubbed his chin with the back of his hand, then worked his jaw back and forth. It wasn't broken, but it hurt like hell. He didn't have any idea how he was going to explain what really happened to Ryder's satisfaction. He still wasn't sure how he and Lynn had ended up in bed together, and he sure didn't want to admit to her brother that it had been a one-night mistake.

Ryder's glare challenged him. He swore, and the words weren't pretty. "We trusted you," he grated. "Hell, Lynn's not even twenty-one."

Russ swallowed hard, forcing the knot in his throat back down. His tanned face reddened. "I know that." The age difference between them stood out like the beam from a lighthouse on a foggy night. Though he'd been aware of Lynn as a young woman for a long time, he'd kept his distance from her. He didn't like how she made him feel, what she'd made him think about. And, hell, now that he'd made love to her, was he ever going to be able to forget?

"Will you two stop talking about me as if I'm not here?" Neither man looked at her. Lynn rolled her eyes and threw her hands in the air with frustration.

"What the hell were you thinking?" Ryder demanded. His heated gaze bore down on Russ, demanding an explanation as he lowered his fisted hands to his sides.

"Ryder!" Lynn scrambled to her knees, still clasping the sheet. "I don't need you to defend my virtue!" she exclaimed, feeling her own temper start to simmer.

"Stay out of this!" Both men shouted the command at the same time.

Feeling disgraced, Russ faced off with Ryder, knowing the entire situation was his fault. During his employment at the ranch, he'd been a trusted employee. He'd worked hard and had proven himself, had just about earned enough money to start a small ranch of his own. Ashley, Ryder's wife, had even gone so far as to mention that she considered him family. Catherine, Jake's new bride, did, too, for that matter.

Well, now he knew which way the wind blew. Ryder was looking at him as if he'd committed the crime of the century. If looks could kill, he'd be dead ten times over. He couldn't believe how much he'd hurt Lynn, how he'd humiliated her by compromising her reputation.

Taking advantage of the silence between the two men, Lynn stated sharply, "Ryder, you idiot, just get out of here. This doesn't concern you!" She yanked at the sheet, struggling wildly until she had it tugged free and pulled around her. With bumbling efforts, she worked herself off the bed and stood.

His eyes still glittering with anger, Ryder pointed his finger at Russ. "Pack your things and get off the ranch!" he ordered, staring him down.

Lynn stormed up to them, her arms tucked tight beside her to keep the sheet in place. "Oh, will you please stop the big brother act?" she cried. "Just mind your own business."

Ryder gave her a brief, silencing glare. "You are my business," he countered hotly. He turned his gaze on Russ again. "And you're fired."

"Oh, puhleeze. I'm not underage, you know." She couldn't believe Russ had been right. If she didn't do some fast talking, this *was* going to cost him his job. "It's not like you're Mister Perfect," she told her brother, her voice slick with sarcasm. Ryder had met

Ashley one night while saving her from the unwanted advances of a drunken cowboy. But he'd ended up stealing her virtue and leaving her pregnant with twins. It had worked out well between them, though, because they'd eventually fallen in love and married. Still, he had no right to be judging her or Russ.

"We're not talking about me or my past deeds," Ryder said in his defense. "We're talking about you." He brought his attention back to Russ. "You've got two hours to be off the ranch."

"Oh, this is ridiculous." She glared at her brother, getting madder by the minute. "Do you have any idea of how stupid you sound?"

"Not nearly as stupid as you look standing there practically naked," he returned, fixing her with a furious stare. "You should be glad I'm the one who found you instead of Jake."

"Now wait just a damn minute," Russ broke in, and his tone lowered dangerously. He wasn't going to just stand there while Ryder berated Lynn. He'd already done enough to hurt her. He couldn't stand knowing he was the reason they were fighting. "Don't talk to her that way," he warned, his expression thunderous. "This isn't Lynn's fault. It's mine." His hard gaze challenged Ryder. Still on edge, he was ready to defend himself if Ryder came at him again.

"You're damn right it is," Ryder agreed, his stance rigid. His hands went to his hips. "I want you off this ranch!"

In a panic, Lynn searched her mind for something, *anything* she could say to save Russ's job. "We're getting married!" she blurted. *Oh, heavens! Had she actually said that out loud?*

She heard Russ's quick intake of breath, and her

head swivelled in his direction. Jeez, she *had* said it! Giving him an encouraging, go-along-with-this look, she moved closer to him, placing her hand possessively on his arm. Her eyes pleaded with him, silencing his protest. "Is that good enough?" she asked her brother, wondering if she'd lost her mind. But it was the only solution she could think of at the moment, the only thing that would save her neck and Russ's job.

His expression questioning, Ryder stared at them both. "You are?" He looked as if he didn't believe her.

Lynn slid closer to Russ, and he put his arm around her. She felt his whole body coil with tension as his hand squeezed her shoulder. "Yes, we just weren't ready to tell anyone yet. We didn't want to take anything away from Jake and Catherine so we kept quiet about our relationship. It wouldn't have been very nice of us to steal their thunder," she told her brother, hoping he wouldn't see through her deception.

Ryder nodded, but still didn't look quite convinced. "You certainly did a great job of keeping this a secret," he stated. He continued to study Russ. "Is this true?" he asked, his tone still obviously suspicious. "Are you going to marry Lynn?" he demanded.

Russ returned an unwavering stare. The fire blazing in his green eyes gave Lynn a cold chill as she waited for him to speak.

"Yes."

Lynn shivered. It wasn't his answer, but his inflexible tone that alarmed her.

"All right, then," Ryder said, still frowning and looking perplexed. His jaw set, he stared at Russ.

"But be warned. You hurt my sister, and there'll be hell to pay."

"Have you ever known me to go back on my word?" Russ challenged.

"Can't say that I have." That said, Ryder's whole demeanor changed. "Look, I apologize for hitting you, Russ. I guess I should've waited for an explanation, but you know how it is. She's my sister."

"Yeah, I know," Russ replied with a nod.

Ryder ruffled his little sister's blond head as if she were a small child. "Damn, Lynn, I don't think anyone expected this," he commented, eyeing her speculatively. Then his mustache quirked up at one corner. "You managed to make everyone think you hated Russ. Sorry, Russ," he said when he saw the foreman's jaw muscle tighten.

Lynn flinched. That was true because she'd believed she had. Now she was so confused. Still, vividly clear shots of the two of them making love kept clicking like slides through her brain, contradicting her previous thoughts and beliefs. The man she'd been with last night had been loving and kind, not abrasive and distant and hard to get along with.

Lynn managed an awkward smile as her gaze found Russ's. She ran her hand along his chest. "Yes, well, we, uh, were quite taken by surprise by our feelings for each other."

"How long has this been going on?" Ryder asked, his gaze sharp and questioning. It was obvious that he was still digesting the news.

"Long enough."

"For a while."

Speaking in unison, Lynn and Russ looked at each other, their eyes locked in a duel. She swallowed a gulp of air as his gaze narrowed. Ryder was watching them both, and Lynn managed a smile when she turned her attention back to him. For a moment, she wasn't certain if her brother wasn't still a little unconvinced. But Russ tugged her closer to him, as if to reassure Ryder of their feelings for each other. His body heat enveloped her, and she swayed, feeling a little light-headed.

Russ shifted his gaze to Ryder. "Look, I'm sorry you had to find out this way, but could you give us a few minutes? We'd like a little privacy, and Lynn needs to dress before we go into any more details."

"Sure thing." Ryder searched around the room for his hat. Spotting it on the floor, he picked it up, then walked to the door.

"Ryder!" Lynn called before he could leave. As he settled his hat on his head, he looked back at her. "Um, could you just give us a little time and not say anything about this to anyone? I'm, uh, we're not quite ready to share this with the family." Her eyes pleaded for a little mercy as she felt Russ's fingers digging into her shoulder.

"You've gotta be kiddin', darlin'," Ryder replied. "What a hoot! You think I'm gonna sit on this and keep it from Ashley?" He snorted a laugh. "She'd kill me." He gave his sister a magnificent grin, then opened the door and walked out, closing it behind him.

"Are you crazy?" Outraged, Russ turned and grabbed Lynn by the shoulders before she could move away.

She blushed. "I'm sorry. It was the first thing that came to my mind." Afraid it would slip, her fingers clutched the sheet tighter. Then the heat of his hands on her skin seeped into her, and it was an effort just to breathe.

"'We're getting married?' *That* was the only thing you could think of?"

"Well, I didn't hear you coming up with any great explanations!" she countered, trying to shrug free.

"Great. Just great." Russ shook his head, trying to make sense of everything, and his hands tightened just a fraction on her shoulders. He couldn't believe what had just happened. In the space of twenty-four hours, he'd made love to Lynn McCall *and* become engaged to her. Could this day get any worse? He let go of her and stormed across the room, his hands on his hips.

"I was trying to save your job!" Lynn yelled, fuming.

So that's what the charade was about, Russ thought, the muscle in his jaw beginning to tick. "That's what you were doing? Saving my job?" He shouldn't feel annoyed that she was admitting she felt nothing for him, but nonetheless it irritated the hell out of him. He'd spent the night making love to her, and this was the second time she'd insisted it meant nothing. He gritted his teeth as the pain of rejection stunned his heart.

Russ turned away from her, unwilling to let her see the wounds she'd opened inside him. He really shouldn't have been surprised. His own mother hadn't wanted him. She'd dumped him with a spinster aunt who'd raised him because of propriety. His wife had cheated on him and had gotten pregnant with her lover's child. Why should Lynn's rejection surprise him or hurt him? It wasn't as if he had delusions about keeping her.

"Yes. You should be thankful, you ingrate," she argued. "Besides, it's not like we're *really* going to get married."

Russ swivelled around and gave a forced laugh. "Oh? And how do you figure that?" he scoffed. He reached up and rubbed his chin with the back of his hand. "By now Ashley knows what happened between us last night, and by this afternoon, everyone who lives on the ranch will know, too."

"So?"

"So, I'm gonna do the right thing and marry you!" Though he knew he'd never have had a chance with Lynn under normal circumstances, he couldn't just stand by and see her reputation ruined. He was duty bound to do right by her, even if it meant that they'd be married only long enough to make it look good.

Lynn went still. "You are not!"

That afforded her a harsh glare. "Oh, yes, I am." His tone was as obstinate as hers, but held underlying menace. Danger lingered in his scorching gaze.

"I don't want to get married to you. We don't even like each other!"

"We *liked* each other well enough last night," he reminded her, his heated gaze running over her skin like warm sunshine.

Lynn felt as if he'd actually touched her. "*That* was just sex." Her tone was defiant.

"It was hot sex, honey. The best sex I've had in a long time."

Her eyes widened as she absorbed the shock of his words. A pleasurable sensation traveled through her. It was on the tip of her tongue to ask him how long, but she caught herself from blurting her thoughts. Instead, she said, "But it was a mistake! It only happened because of the circumstances last night that led up to it.'' Her voice shook slightly, and she stared at him.

''A mistake?'' His laugh was wry. He knew when a woman was naturally responding to him, and Lynn was all over him last night. ''A few beers and a little champagne were the reasons you responded so eagerly when I made love to you?'' He regarded her silently and struggled with the effort to keep his temper under control. ''So, you're saying now, in the light of day and without the mood of last night and a little alcohol, you wouldn't respond the same way?''

''I'm saying it doesn't matter.'' Her voice lost some of its boldness as she adjusted the sheet, tucking it under her arms so that it wouldn't come loose.

''It doesn't?'' One of his eyebrows quirked up.

''Last night is over. This engagement between us is a *pretend* engagement.''

''Were you pretending last night?'' Russ demanded, still annoyed that she could dismiss what happened between them so easily.

''I—''

''Are you saying you were pretending when you begged me to come inside you?''

''Russ, please—''

''When you screamed my name and came apart in my arms?'' he asked, studying her. ''Lynn, honey, you're lying.''

''Oh, no, I'm not,'' she declared, clasping her hands together to keep them from shaking. How had she let him back her into a corner over this? She didn't want to argue with him. She had her own agenda—starting her own horse ranch. Growing up under the control of three older brothers while trying to assert her independence had been difficult, and she just wanted a chance to prove herself. Though she knew her brothers loved her and wanted what was best for her, Lynn was ready to think for herself, make her own decisions.

And she didn't *want* to be attracted, physically or otherwise, to Russ Logan.

"Prove it."

"What?" she gulped.

Russ let his gaze slowly slide over her. "Come over here and prove it, honey," he said evenly, the determination inside him fueled by her persistence that what happened between them was a fluke and by the fact that he was now *engaged* to her.

She retreated a step, then silently cursed herself for it. "I will not!"

Russ pinned her gaze with his. "Come over here now, Lynn."

"No."

His jaw muscle twitched as he walked over to her. Without speaking, he touched her chin with his finger and lifted her face so he could look into her eyes.

"Come on, honey, show me how much you *don't* want me."

He moved closer, crowding her space. Trapped, Lynn felt the bed behind her legs, preventing her from moving. Russ lifted his hand and gently stroked her neck with the back of his fingers. Her eyelids closed as pleasure began a torturous flow through her body.

"Kiss me," he commanded.

"No," she answered, opening her eyes slowly and looking at him. Her answer held little conviction as awareness tightened the tension between them. The air in the room became thick and heavy, making it hard to breathe. She leaned toward him, her nipples hardening beneath the sheet as her breasts swelled.

"Kiss me," he said again, dropping his hand away from her.

Though his words were still a command, they came out sounding more like temptation. Lynn opened her mouth to tell him no again and felt his hot breath skim her lips. Her lungs seemed starved for air. He didn't touch her, but, oh, how she wanted him to. Her entire body tightened with desire as the heat of his skin penetrated hers, luring her closer.

Her teeth clinched her bottom lip as she looked at his mouth. She licked her lips, and she didn't know how he managed it, but he moved closer, aligning his body with hers so that they touched from chest to knees. The friction between them felt like icy fire.

"Show me," he whispered, then he bent his head toward her. Her lips parted, and he caught her lower lip with his teeth, biting it gently, then letting it go. "Show me, honey," he whispered.

"Russ." Lynn raised her hands, but instead of using them to push him away, she slid them over his bare chest, then up to his cheeks, holding his face near hers. "This is insane." Her words came out in a rush of breath. Seeing he wasn't going to let it go, she gave in and brushed her mouth against his.

What started as a simple kiss changed so suddenly that Lynn didn't have time to think. All she could comprehend was the vortex of need that consumed her as his tongue invaded her mouth, touching the tip of hers.

Someone groaned. Lynn thought it was her, but she wasn't sure, wasn't aware of anything except the heady feel of Russ's lips on hers, the pressure of his hard body as she moved closer to him. She lifted her mouth from his, caught her breath in a snatched moment, then she pressed her mouth against his again. Her hands slid to his neck and tightened, and she strained on her toes to fuse her lips against his.

Finally, he pulled away from her and she opened her eyes. Everything inside her had shifted. Her wants, her needs, her focus. What had happened? Though she felt as if she'd been ravaged, she realized he hadn't even touched her. His hands were still hanging by his side. She was shocked and quite embarrassed that it was her, not Russ, who appeared so moved by their kisses.

"This, um, doesn't prove anything," she said, pulling her hands away from him. She scooted around him and started to gather her clothes. Bending down she snatched up her blue dress.

Stepping back a little, Russ grinned lasciviously. "Yeah, right." Oh, he was in trouble. If he'd kissed her any longer, he'd have pulled the sheet off of her, pushed her down on the bed and taken her again.

Furious at her response to him, she straightened and squared her shoulders. Then, out of the blue, another disturbing thought hit her.

"Condoms!" Her eyes widened, and she drew in a sharp breath as she ran to the bed. Clutching the sheet to help keep it in place, she whipped the remaining tangled covers from the bed and tossed the pillows willy-nilly. "Oh...dammit!" Dropping to her knees, she threw herself on the floor and searched beneath the bed for torn-open empty packets. Then she came up slowly, her head showing first, her eyes filled with dread.

"We didn't use any protection, did we?" she wailed.

His expression deeply regretful, Russ shook his head. "Not that I remember," he admitted, confirming the worst.

He usually always took precautions.

Always.

Except last night.

Lynn sank onto the bed, then bent forward, holding her head with her hand. "Oh no, no, no."

Russ walked over to her, not believing he'd caused yet another complication. He just couldn't get a break here. "Damn, Lynn, I don't know what to say, except that I really screwed up." That was an understatement of humongous proportions.

"You mean *we* screwed up."

Russ grunted. "I'm the one who should've been concerned with protecting you," he insisted. "I don't usually drink enough to cloud my brain. Last night was an exception, rather than a rule." He looked down at her, feeling like a fool. "It doesn't matter, anyway. Since we're getting married, it'll be all right if you're pregnant."

Three

"**I** am not going to be pregnant!" She said it with confirmation, staring steadfastly at him. "And I am not going to marry you!"

Russ's lips thinned, and his green eyes glittered. "Yes, you are." His tone made it sound like a done deal.

"No, I'm not!" She almost stamped her foot, but quickly realized how childish it would appear.

He bent down toward her, putting his face so close in front of hers that she could see the tiny veins in his eyes. "I...don't...lie."

She jerked her head back. "What?"

"I gave your brother my word, and I mean to abide by it. *You* are the one who forced this issue, and you're just gonna have to live with whatever problem you created."

Though momentarily impressed by his integrity,

she wasn't going to let him bully her. "We'll think of something. Wait, I know!" she said in a rush. "We'll pretend for a while we're getting married, just long enough to be sure I'm not pregnant, which, I repeat, is not going to happen. As soon as we know for sure I'm not, then we'll stage a fight and break off our engagement."

"That's ridiculous. Your brothers aren't gonna fall for that," Russ scoffed.

"Let's not worry about it right now. For the moment, Ryder's happy, and you have your job. That's the important thing." Darting around him as well as she could with the sheet around her legs and feet, Lynn hurriedly gathered her clothing. "In the meantime, I'm getting dressed and getting out of here."

Russ bit his tongue. He started to push his argument with her, then stopped himself. In a short time she'd realize just how serious he was. He'd given Ryder his word. He wasn't going back on it, no matter what she said. "Fine."

She snapped her head around and looked up at him, and a flush gave her cheeks a rosy tone. "Fine." She walked toward the bathroom. "I'll be out of your hair in a few minutes." Stepping inside, she closed the door behind her, then wished she could sink into the earth and disappear.

We're getting married!

What *had* she been thinking? Jeez, having an impulsive nature, she'd been known to put her foot in her mouth more than once, something her three brothers had teased her about more often than not. But this time she'd really done it.

Okay, maybe she had spoken hastily, but she didn't understand Russ's hostile attitude. He sure as heck didn't seem to appreciate her idea of breaking up a pretend engagement, either. Instead of fighting her on it, the man should have been thanking her for saving his job!

He'd looked positively thunderous and intimidating moments ago when he'd said he was going to marry her. A chuckle escaped her lips as she slid on her panties and bra, then arranged the dress so she could slip it over her head.

What a ridiculous thought! She and Russ getting married. Lord have mercy, the last thing she wanted was to be tied down with a husband. She'd lived with her three older brothers telling her what to do her entire life. Now that she was old enough to make her own decisions, she certainly wasn't going to do something stupid like get married and let another man tell her what she could and couldn't do. She wasn't going to throw away her hopes and dreams.

Now, honestly, she'd have to admit that being with Russ last night *had* been something she'd never forget. She shivered as she remembered the delicious sensation of him stroking her body with his big hands and the tantalizing feel of his tongue on her skin. The taste of him still lingered in her mind. Being initiated into lovemaking by Russ had definitely been the high point of her life.

But as wonderful as it had felt being with him, it wasn't real. They weren't in love, or for that matter, anything close to it. Heavens, all of this fuss just because she'd made a little mistake. Well, maybe sleeping with Russ *was* more than just a little mistake, she amended silently, struggling to zip up the back of her dress.

She looked in the mirror and studied her image as

memories of being in his arms continued to taunt her. Did she look any different, she wondered? She shook her head as if to shake away the thought. No, of course not. That flush in her cheeks was from embarrassment—not from learning what it was like to have a man make love to her.

Or to have Russ Logan make love to you.

Frowning, she looked down at the bathroom counter and picked up a bottle of his cologne. She sniffed at the cap, and the scent of him filled her senses. She closed her eyes and the memory of feeling him moving inside her assaulted her. She swayed, then put her hand against the counter, catching herself.

Oh, heavens! How could she face him day after day after what they'd done last night?

She opened her eyes and stared at herself. Okay, she'd just have to grin and bear it. Seeing him every day would get easier, right? Eventually, it would be as if it had never happened.

Squaring her shoulders, she brushed her hands through her hair, but it still looked quite mussed. Grabbing Russ's comb, she ran it through her hair several times, giving it some order. Using a piece of bathroom tissue, she wiped traces of her tears from under her eyes.

She took a deep breath, deciding she was looking as good as she was going to under the circumstances. As she opened the bathroom door, her gaze landed on Russ. He hadn't moved. He was staring at her, his jaw set tight, his expression just as rigid.

"I'll, uh, just get out of here," she said, frowning and looking away. Russ didn't say a word. Swallowing past the knot in her throat, Lynn looked around the room for her heels. She spotted them on the floor at the foot of the bed. Quickly, she walked over and scooped them up, then went to the door. But she couldn't bring herself to just walk out as if nothing had happened between them. As much as she wanted to ignore it, there was no disputing that they'd crossed an invisible line in their working relationship.

Still, what could she say? By the way, thanks for giving me a night I'll never forget? While she'd never really gotten along with Russ, she'd always been aware of his masculinity, of his virility. She'd just never dreamed he'd be the man who'd teach her about making love. Nor had she any idea that making love with him would make her so aware of her own sexuality.

Turning to face Russ, she caught her bottom lip with her teeth. "Um, I guess I'll be seeing you. I'm, uh, sorry about all this. I mean, the trouble and everything."

Russ's expression relaxed a fraction. Damn her! She looked so adorable trying to say something that wouldn't sound awkward. But there was nothing either of them could say to make this all go away.

The damage was done. She was going to have to face it. Instead of challenging her, he decided to let her go, knowing she'd soon realize just how serious he was about doing the honorable thing and marrying her.

"Yeah. I'm sorry, too," he said quietly.

But as she walked out the door and closed it behind her, he knew he wasn't sorry about everything. He was sorry as hell that he'd messed up. He was sorry he'd taken her virginity when under normal circumstances, he'd have never allowed himself to get close enough to her for that to be a possibility.

He wasn't sorry he knew what it was like to make love to her.

As he walked into the bathroom to shower, Russ thought about the position they were in. Maybe Lynn didn't think marriage was a good idea, but he knew it was the only answer. He didn't give his word lightly. Ryder had looked him directly in the eyes and asked if Russ was going to marry his sister. Unable to lie about the situation, Russ had gone along with Lynn's ruse, knowing in his heart that he'd meant it.

Turning on the shower, he adjusted the water temperature and stepped inside, letting the hot spray cover his body. He knew he was in dangerous territory. He'd made up his mind a long time ago not to get emotionally involved with another woman, and until he'd ended up in bed with Lynn McCall, he'd had no trouble sticking to his plans to remain single and detached.

His wife had taught him a hard lesson, but he'd been a quick learner. Her rejection had stung, but it had also toughened his skin. Despite what had happened between him and Lynn, he wasn't going to allow her close enough to hurt him. He had a suspicious feeling that if he did, her rejection would hurt ten times more than Candace's.

Looking back at his past, he'd married Candace because he'd been searching for the American dream—a house, a loving wife, a family. Not that he hadn't cared for her—he had, as much as he'd allowed himself to. And apparently his feelings for her had been a hell of a lot deeper than hers for him.

While he'd been busy building them a secure life to-gether, she'd been running around on him.

Well, hell, he didn't need more sorrow, didn't need a fresh taste of feminine rejection. His relationship with Candace had left a bitter taste in his mouth that hadn't diminished despite the years that had passed. He wasn't going to put his heart on the line for Lynn McCall to stomp on. He'd keep his emotions out of this dilemma.

Reaching over and turning off the water, he re-minded himself that his emotions really had little to do with it. He'd given his word. That was basically the story in a nutshell. His heart wasn't in danger because he wasn't in love with Lynn. Even if he mar-ried her, he'd keep it that way. Besides, he knew it wouldn't be a forever-after kind of relationship. Hell, it wouldn't even be a real marriage.

Of course, if she was pregnant with his child, that would change the stakes quite a bit. But what were the chances of that happening? As he dried off and began to dress, he berated himself for putting her at risk. Crockett was a town where everyone knew each other. The people were far from liberal, and they had their share of meddlers who would jump on the tiniest tidbit of information, turn it into a scandal and feed on it for months. He hated thinking he would be the one responsible for starting rumors about Lynn.

Pulling on his jeans, he tucked in his black short-sleeved shirt, then buckled his belt. He sat down on the bed and yanked on his socks and boots. After slapping on some cologne and combing his hair, he grabbed his hat and left his quarters, then headed across the wide, dusty yard to the main house where the McCall family lived.

Though it was the end of summer, Mother Nature apparently hadn't noticed. The hot, Texas sun baked down on him, and he was nearly working up a sweat as he approached the house. The ranch-style structure was massive, and there was an ongoing construction project creating a new wing for Ryder, Ashley and their babies. Shaking his head, Russ chuckled to himself. Ryder had sworn he'd never marry and here he was about to have his third child in little over a year!

Taking the wooden porch steps two at a time, Russ stopped at the front door. Though he'd often been told to come in without knocking, it had never quite felt right. He hesitated briefly, then rapped his knuckles solidly on the screen door. A moment later, Ashley swung open the front door.

"Russ!" Her big brown eyes lit with excitement as they met his. "Ryder told me the news. Oh, my goodness, Russ Logan, you get in here and give me a hug!" Her grin was as welcoming as a cool breeze on a sweltering summer night.

Before Russ had a chance to prepare himself, she flung the screen door open and reached for him, pulling him as close as she could due to her enlarged belly. She was so exuberant, he had to put his arms around her to steady her. When she finally let him go, he stepped back and slowly met her gaze. Her eyes were shining as though she'd discovered the secret to a lifetime of happiness.

"Oh my gosh! You and Lynn getting married," she went on, not giving him a chance to speak. "I'm so happy for you both." Grabbing his arm, she looped hers through it and drew him toward the large den.

Russ gave her a slight nod and a forced grin. "Thanks," was all he could manage to say. He and

Lynn still had a lot to discuss, and he'd been hoping she'd be the one to greet him at the door. He wasn't sure what he should be saying to Ashley and figured the less said, the better.

Matt, Jake's twelve-year-old son, came rushing past them, knocking into Russ as he raced toward the door. "Oops! Sorry, Russ," he said, breathing hard. "Ryder said I could go along with him while he was working today if I could get ready and be outside in time. Gotta go." He raced out the door and took off toward the barn.

"He's settled in nicely, hasn't he?" Russ commented, not really expecting an answer.

"Quicker than anyone expected," Ashley agreed. "He's a great kid, and despite the fact that there was only his mother and him for so long, he appears to love being a part of a large family." As soon as they walked into the den, two dark-headed babies crawled over to them as fast as they could move.

The next thing Russ knew, one of the babies, Melissa, he thought, was tugging on his leg in an effort to pull up and stand on her feet. Automatically, he bent down and picked her up. Though the twins looked alike, their personalities were very different. Melissa loved everyone, but Michelle tended to prefer her mom and dad's attention.

"Catherine and Jake are sure to be surprised when they hear the news about you and Lynn. I can't wait for them to return from their honeymoon," Ashley remarked, picking up Michelle. She kissed the top of the baby's head.

"Yeah," Russ muttered, trying his best to remain evasive as he studied Melissa's smiling face. As he looked at the baby, he thought about Lynn. She could be carrying his child right now! His heart jumped at the thought.

When he'd left Candace, he'd made up his mind that he'd never give his heart to another woman, which pretty much sealed his fate as far as having children was concerned. He thought he'd adjusted to the idea that he'd never be a father.

The possibility of Lynn being pregnant brought his earlier desires for a home and family to the surface. Though he didn't really *want* her to be pregnant, he couldn't deny the longing he felt inside. But he quashed it before he let his mind run with it, knowing it would be ridiculous for him to entertain such a foolish notion.

Lynn might have made love with him, but if she'd been in her right mind, she'd never have ended up in his bed. He couldn't forget that.

"To tell you the truth, I've sort of suspected that maybe you and Lynn had feelings for each other," Ashley commented, interrupting his thoughts.

Russ's head whipped around, and his eyes connected with hers. "What?" He couldn't possibly have heard right. What would make Ashley think that? he wondered.

"Oh, come on, Russ," she told him, a teasing smile on her lips. "You and Lynn have had more confrontations than a bull and a matador. I just couldn't help suspecting that there was something brewing between you two."

The muscle in his jaw worked back and forth. He couldn't really deny what Ashley was implying without giving away his and Lynn's secret that last night was the first time they'd ever been together. And he hated not being totally truthful. Damn Lynn for getting him into this mess! And where the hell was she anyway?

Gritting his teeth, he glanced toward the doorway leading to the hall and bedrooms. "Is she around?" he asked, sounding impatient even though he was trying his best to act as if his whole life hadn't been turned upside down.

"I think she's dressing. She should be done any minute."

Ashley sat on the sofa, then motioned for Russ to take a seat. He politely declined, preferring to stand. He couldn't sit still. He felt jumpy inside, as if all his emotions were bouncing around like heated molecules. He couldn't get a grip on relaxing because all he could think about was Lynn and how she made him feel.

"You know, this really is exciting," Ashley went on. "Ryder and I had an impromptu wedding, as did Catherine and Jake. It'll be fun to plan a really big wedding for a change." Russ frowned, and she chuckled. "It won't be too bad, I promise." Hearing footsteps, she turned her head toward the door.

Lynn walked into the room, then stopped suddenly when she saw Russ. He took one look at her and felt as if he'd received a hard punch to his gut. Gone was the beautiful, sexy woman he'd spent the night loving. In her place he saw the young woman he'd watched grow and change over the time he'd been working at the Bar M.

She had on worn, snug-fitting blue jeans, along with a blue-flowered tank top that hugged her breasts. His gaze strayed to them and stayed there a moment too long, long enough for him to remember what it felt like to lick them with his tongue, suck her nipples

into his mouth. Feeling his body grow hard with desire, he stepped behind the sofa. Jerking his gaze back
to hers, he swallowed hard and wondered where in
the world his good sense had disappeared to.

He shouldn't be thinking about Lynn like that, but
he just couldn't help it. One night with her had given
him an idea of what it would be like to make love to
her for the rest of his life.

Don't go there. Don't torture yourself.

He wasn't the right man for Lynn, and he damn
well knew it. Just because their sexual chemistry was
right, didn't mean they were right for each other in
all the other ways where it counted.

Besides, he'd never be able to give her his heart.
Lynn deserved a hell of a lot more from the man she'd
spend the rest of her life with.

What he should be thinking about was the problem
at hand. He'd go along with her on the engagement
for a while, until he could marry her like he'd promised. But he'd damn sure keep his hands off of her
from now on.

"Oh, hey, Lynn," Ashley said, greeting her sister-
in-law. "I was just telling Russ how much fun it'll
be to plan a real wedding. By the way, have you two
decided on a date?"

"A date?" Lynn repeated, sounding confused.

"Yes, silly girl, a date!" When Lynn still didn't
respond, Ashley added in a prompting tone, "for the
wedding."

Panic-stricken, Russ unconsciously clutched the
baby in his arms a little tighter. His gaze confronted
Lynn's across the room. He could see that she was
thinking of something to say, but he wasn't sure what
would come out of her mouth.

"We haven't decided on a date yet," he stated quickly, trying to think of something that would throw Ashley off track. "We didn't want to horn in on Catherine and Jake's impending nuptials. But now that they're married and the cat's out of the bag, so to speak, we're on our way to San Luis to pick out a ring."

Surprise registered on Lynn's face a split second before she concealed it and shot him a warning look. Despite her attempt to smile, her lips thinned. Well, that was just tough. She was the one responsible for this whole fiasco, not him.

"Are you ready to go?" he asked, moving toward her with Melissa in his arms. Stopping close to her, he put his arm around her shoulders while he held the baby against his chest.

"A...ring?" she asked, and her voice cracked.

"Sure, honey. Remember we talked about it this morning?" Russ said smoothly, trying his best to appear normal and encouraging her to also. She seemed small and fragile standing next to him, and he felt her whole body tremble.

Lynn forced a smile to her lips. Though she was so angry it was a miracle smoke wasn't coming out of her ears, she tried her best to appear happy. "Oh, um, yes."

Russ looked at Ashley. "Where should I deposit this little one?" he asked, nodding at Melissa. Ashley leaned over and put Michelle on the floor, then told Russ to do the same with Melissa. He stepped away from Lynn long enough to put the baby down, then straightened and reached for Lynn's hand. Grasping it firmly, he tugged her toward the door.

"We'll see you later, Ashley," he called over his shoulder.

Lynn tried to pull her hand away, and Russ shot her a hard glare. She relented, not wanting to make a scene in front of her sister-in-law. She quickly said goodbye and let Russ lead her out the door. But she had no intention of going anywhere with him, and that especially included picking out an engagement ring!

Once they were outside and alone, Russ practically dragged her down the steps. "Will you come on?" he bit out, turning around and facing her.

"Let me go!" Lynn rasped, fuming.

Russ stopped, but firmly held on to her hand. "No. I'm not going to stand here and make a scene in front of Ashley or anyone else within hearing distance. You've caused enough havoc in my life right now without adding more!"

"Me?" Lynn shot back, her lips twisting with anger. "*You're* the one who just told Ashley that we're going to get a ring."

"Well, what else could I say?" he retorted. He started walking, heading across the yard to his truck, pulling her along with him. "You were the one who told your brother we're getting married. Besides, what if you're pregnant?" They rounded the back of the building where he lived, and he stopped beside his black pickup.

"Shhh!" Lynn grated in a hushed tone. "Lower your voice!" She glanced around and was relieved that no one was near enough to have overheard him. "Do you want everyone to know that's a possibility?"

Russ flashed her a regretful frown. "Sorry. I'm just

trying to do the right thing here. You told Ryder we're getting married. He and Ashley think we're engaged. Before long, other people will, too. So we're going to get a ring. Otherwise, everyone will wonder why you aren't wearing one,'' he reasoned.

Lynn felt panic rise inside her. She hadn't thought of that. This whole thing was getting way out of hand. She'd only been trying to save Russ's job, and now they were in a huge mess that was getting deeper and deeper. He opened the door for her and indicated for her to get in. Feeling as though she was losing control of her life, Lynn hesitated.

''Look, like I said, you created this farce. Now we're both gonna have to live with it until, as you said, we figure a way out of it.'' And to Russ, that meant he was going to marry her. He'd promised. He wasn't going back on his word. ''Now, get in the truck.''

Lynn glared at him with fire in her eyes. She started to get in, then stopped and turned, and her hot gaze confronted his. ''Listen, and listen good. You and everyone else had better understand something. Don't take this personally, but I have plans to live my life my own way—and they *don't* include a husband. Not now or anytime in the near future!''

Four

As Russ went around the pickup and got in behind the wheel, Lynn made work of buckling her seat belt. Heat had built up inside the cab, and the air was stifling, already causing her blouse to stick to her skin. She fanned herself with her hand as he fastened himself in. With jerky movements, he started the engine, then switched on the air-conditioning. Shifting the truck into gear, he pulled away from the ranch.

As he concentrated on driving, Lynn looked over at him. His worn jeans gloved his body, and she thought his shirt matched his dark mood. A week ago—even the day before yesterday—she might not have admitted it, but he was one handsome man. His presence beside her was staggering, heightening all her senses, putting all her nerves on extreme alert. It was as if she'd just had her eyes opened for the first time and realized how incredibly sexy and masculine he was. Now she was afraid that she'd never be able to forget.

Glancing out the window, she tried to focus on her surroundings, but was unable to stop thinking about how being intimate with Russ had affected her. She just hadn't expected him to be the first person she'd see after she'd showered and changed. After leaving his quarters, she'd felt a sense of relief. She'd dreaded facing him again, though she'd known she would have to and it would be awkward.

All right, if she was honest with herself, she'd also been anxious and a little bit excited. Her gaze strayed to him again, taking in his long, tanned arms sprinkled with a dusting of dark hair, then lingered on his strong hands gripping the steering wheel. His white knuckles indicated that he wasn't feeling at ease either.

She knew how he felt. Her mind and body seemed in turmoil. Though she knew better than to let herself become further involved with Russ, she couldn't help remembering how wonderful it felt to be loved by him. She couldn't forget his kisses or the way he made her feel when he touched her.

Bringing her thoughts back to the present, she twisted her hands in her lap. She hadn't meant to get them in such a bind, but he hadn't really helped by stating they were going to get a ring. Frustrated, she sighed heavily as she turned her head away and glanced out the window. They passed one of the fenced pastures where a group of horses were grazing. There was so much work to do. It seemed a shame to waste the day riding into San Luis to get a ring that she didn't want, wasn't going to wear and was going to return.

"This is really a waste of time," she stated, giving him a defiant look.

Russ grimaced, holding himself in check. "I said we're going to get a ring, and that's what we're gonna do."

"Because you say so?" she challenged.

He gave her a direct look. "No," he said very carefully, "because *you* blurted out that we're getting married."

"There's no need for you to spend money on a ring," she insisted. "It's a *pretend* engagement."

Russ swallowed hard. Lynn was testing his patience, which was wearing very thin at the moment. "Then think of it as a *pretend* ring," he told her, his tone flat and uncompromising.

"Look," she argued, turning in her seat to face him, "don't you see that a ring is going to just add credence to this whole situation? It's going to make it seem, I don't know, more official." He didn't seem to be listening to her, and she had a feeling that her reasoning was falling on deaf ears. She was quickly learning that Russ Logan had a mind of his own. Well, he was going to have to learn that she wasn't going to jump at his every command.

"That's the point of getting it. I've already told you how it's going to look if I don't put a ring on your finger." Silence fell between them. Russ wasn't about to defend his actions again. She wasn't ready to face the fact that they were going to have to pay for their night of passion. He could understand her hesitation about marrying him since she'd just told him in no uncertain terms that she had no plans to take a husband.

Well, he hadn't planned on getting married again

either. Because his first marriage had turned out
badly, he figured he just didn't have what it took to
make a permanent relationship work.

That was before last night, before he'd made love
to Lynn, before he'd taken her virginity. He stole a
glance at her, and a part of him wished things were
different, that he had something to offer her. She was
leaning against the door of the truck, her legs crossed,
her lips in a full pout. His gaze dropped to her breasts,
and he wanted like hell to touch her there. His body
responded quickly to his thoughts, and he turned his
attention back to the road.

He was going to have to get his libido under control. He couldn't go around lusting after Lynn until
this whole farce was over. The problem was it was
going to be a strain trying to distance himself physically. Just being with her reminded him of what it
had been like to hold her in his arms, to kiss her
beautiful, tempting lips.

"What about yourself? This has all been about me
and my reputation, which you and Ryder are more
worried about than I am."

"What do you mean?"

Unable to suppress her curiosity, she asked,
"Aren't there women, I mean, isn't there a woman in
your life that's gonna be disappointed that she's not
the one you're going to marry?" She'd been wanting
to ask, but the opportunity hadn't presented itself.

"No."

His abrupt answer caused her to raise her eyebrows.
"No? Really?"

He flashed her a tolerant look. "No one you need
to concern yourself about."

What did that mean? Lynn wondered. That he had

women whom he saw on occasion, but no one special? Or that his female companionship wasn't up for
discussion?

"What about you?"

"I'm not seeing anyone. I told you, I don't want
any commitments right now."

He seemed to mull that over, and they fell silent
for a while as they headed away from the small town
of Crockett and toward Ozona on Interstate 10. Russ
gunned the engine to pick up speed.

"What kind of plans?"

Startled from the sudden sound of his voice, she
jumped, then she looked at him. He glanced briefly
at her, then just as quickly away.

"What?"

"You said you had plans and that you don't want
any commitments. What kind of plans?"

His tone was gruff, as if idle conversation didn't
come easily to him. Though not really talkative, it
seemed he got along well with everyone at the Bar
M, except her. They'd never had a real conversation
that she could remember that hadn't ended up in some
kind of disagreement. Surprised by his interest, wondering if it was genuine, she flushed a little.

"Oh, um, I've been thinking a lot about what I
want to do. I love working with horses so I'm going
to start my own horse ranch." Why had she even told
him? She hadn't shared her plans with her brothers
yet for fear that they wouldn't take her seriously. At
least Jake and Ryder wouldn't. After arriving at the
house this morning, she'd learned that Deke had left
as soon as dawn broke to go back on the rodeo circuit.
Lynn didn't think he was too concerned about anything except competing.

"You want to start a horse ranch?" Even though he made an effort at it, Russ couldn't conceal his skepticism. Starting a ranch of any kind was long, hard, backbreaking work. He doubted Lynn had any idea of how difficult it was to begin such a venture, let alone be a success at it.

Lynn crossed her arms over her chest. "Yes," she replied tersely, giving him an annoyed look. "Despite what you think of me, I'm very good with horses."

Russ flinched. He guessed he deserved that. He had given her a rough time since they'd started working together. But that wasn't his fault. It was Jake's. He'd told Russ to work Lynn hard, to give her menial tasks. Her brother wanted her to give up the idea of training horses and quit. Jake still wanted Lynn to go to college.

Russ figured that was because Jake hadn't had an opportunity to finish school. When his parents had been killed in a plane crash, he'd had to leave school, come back home and raise his younger siblings. He'd mentioned to Russ that he wanted at least one of his siblings to get a college degree. Ryder hadn't gone, and Deke was more interested in competing in the rodeo. Considering what Lynn had just divulged, she didn't plan on listening to her brother about continuing her education, either.

"I wasn't implying that you weren't," Russ said, and swallowed hard.

"It sure sounded like it."

"I'll admit you've learned a lot. You have a natural instinct with horses, that's for sure," he offered. He didn't want to encourage her, but he wasn't going to lie to her either. Working with her had taught him a thing or two about her. She was smart and had an intuitive talent with horses. Anyone with a lick of sense could see that much about her if they watched her train.

He'd even pointed it out to Jake a time or two. And she didn't give up. No matter what Russ had given her to do, she'd done it. Sometimes with a lot of sass, he thought, stifling a smile, but she'd stuck it out.

Lynn sat up straighter and turned in her seat toward him. "Careful with those compliments. I might faint." His dark look almost made her smile. "Jake is having a hard time letting go. He still wants me to go to college, and I'm tired of fighting with him."

"He only wants what's best for you," Russ told her patiently.

"I know, but I'm hoping now that he's married and has a child of his own, he'll get off my case." The more Lynn thought about them, the more sure she was of her plans. Jake would be busy with his own family now. He wouldn't have as much time to worry about her.

Matthew, Jake's son, had shown up at the ranch without warning, claiming that Jake was his father. Catherine, Matt's mother and Jake's college sweetheart, had come to the ranch to get him, and she and Jake had ended up falling in love again. Lynn was happy they'd found each other again after all the years that had passed. She was equally glad that Matt was Jake's natural son. Her brother had been in an accident shortly after he'd returned to the ranch after their parents' death, and he'd learned he'd never be able to father a child. Now he had a family, and he'd never seemed happier.

"He'll have his hands full, that's for sure," Russ agreed. "It's a good thing Ryder had started the addition to the house. Although it's already big, it's hard for two families to share the same space.''

"That's another reason I want my own place," Lynn confided. "It's not that I don't love my family, because I do. They mean a lot to me. And I adore Ryder and Ashley's twins, but Michelle and Melissa will be walking soon, so when Ryder and his family move into the new wing when it's finished, I think it'll be nice for Jake, Catherine and Matt to have the rest of the house."

"Wanting your own ranch is one thing, Lynn, making a go of it is another," Russ warned. "Do you have any idea of how hard it'll be to start a ranch? It's tough enough for a man."

Lynn glared at him. "Meaning?"

Russ took the main exit off the interstate leading to San Luis. "Meaning it'll be twice as hard for a woman to start a ranch and make it a success. Just ask Mary Beth Adams," he told her, thinking of the McCalls' neighbor. She'd recently lost her father, and she was trying to keep their ranch going on her own. "Jake sends one or two of the hands over to her place to help her out all the time."

"She's just having a rough time," Lynn reasoned. "Once she gets straightened out, she can hire a couple of hands." His reminder of Mary Beth's struggles struck home. Lynn was sure that once she announced her plans, Jake would certainly use Mary Beth's struggles as an argument against her idea to start her own ranch. She'd have to be careful and prepare herself for his arguments.

"What other plans have you made?" he asked. It surprised him to learn that they actually had something in common. The spread he'd purchased was small in comparison to the land the McCalls owned, but it was enough for him. All he needed was a little more money for livestock. And he needed his job at the Bar M to earn that. Then he could get his own place off the ground.

"Well, first, I figured we've got plenty of land, so I could just pick out a few acres and stake my claim to them. And I'm planning to go and see Linwood Finney at the bank with a financial plan. He's known my family for ages, and he knows I'd be good for the loan. I've already sketched out some basic building plans. I want to start small and grow slowly. I could continue living at the Bar M while I get the ranch off the ground, then move once I have a small house built."

She continued describing her plans, her face animated and full of excitement as she shared her thoughts, her dreams. Russ was impressed. He admired her tenacity and spunk. She'd thought it all out, had a financial plan and the drive to make it happen. He didn't think her brothers were going to like it one bit, but he didn't voice his thoughts. No need to shoot holes in her plans. There were still a few obstacles in her way, their engagement and impending marriage being the biggest ones.

Russ chewed a bit on the inside of his mouth as he slowed the truck down and pulled into the parking lot of the mall at San Luis. Essentially, what Lynn had said was true. She had plans, and they didn't include a husband. Whether he was right for her or not, it was clear she wasn't interested in him. That's why she was so intent on a pretend engagement, he thought, his mood darkening. She was determined to follow her own agenda. Though he knew there could never be anything serious between them, her rejection deepened the hole in his heart, stung in a way that his mother's and Candace's hadn't.

He figured Jake was going to somehow figure this was partly Russ's fault. He was supposed to work with her on training the horses, bringing her along slowly. He'd tried, but Lynn had picked up on every tiny detail while they worked together. She was smart and thorough. Hell, for all he knew, she probably could make a go of running her own place.

If Jake gave her the chance.

Turning his thoughts to the matter at hand, he pulled the truck to a stop in a parking spot. "We're here," he stated matter-of-factly.

"Russ—"

"Don't even start," he warned her, getting out of the truck. He walked around to open her door, but she was already climbing out. She slammed the door and came toward him.

"I'm sorry," Lynn said. "I know you mean well, but I just can't go through with this!" she insisted. His sense of honor was amazing, his tenacity more on the order of irritating.

Russ took her hand and held it tightly. "You can, and you will. Come on." He tugged her into the mall and down one of the wide hallways, passing by clothing stores, a toy store and a specialty chocolate shop. "There's got to be a jewelry store in here somewhere." He wanted his ring on Lynn's finger before Jake and Catherine returned. Facing one of her brothers without his intentions known had been hard enough.

"I've been here lots of times," Lynn insisted, "and I don't remember one." She finished speaking just as they were turning a corner. Russ stopped in his tracks, and she bumped right into him. He turned, and as she stepped back, gave her a hard stare.

"Oh? So, what's this?" he asked, his tone sarcastic. They were standing in front of a small, but well-known jewelry store. "A figment of my imagination?"

Lynn tugged on her hand. "I'm not going in there with you!" Even as she said the words, he let go of her hand, slid his arm behind her back and propelled her forward. The touch of his hand against her sent a rush of awareness throughout her entire body, zapping her resistance. Grimacing, she told herself she had to work on her self-control. She just couldn't turn to jelly every time he touched her.

A well-dressed woman approached them as soon as they entered. "May I help you?" she asked, a polite and welcoming smile on her lips.

Russ nodded. "Yes, ma'am. We're here to pick out an engagement ring." Somehow Lynn had managed to disengage herself from him, and he grabbed her by the arm and pulled her to him, this time holding her a little closer to keep her next to him. "This is my fiancée," he said.

The woman's smile turned brighter. "Oh, wonderful! Do you have any idea of the kind of ring you're interested in? We have some beautiful diamonds, and of course, other precious stones if you're looking for something unique." She urged them to follow her, then she stepped behind a counter and faced them. Using a key to open it, she withdrew part of the display and placed it on the counter. An array of sparkling diamonds glistened against dark, midnight blue velvet.

Russ looked at Lynn. "Which one do you like?"

Aghast at the selection, she shook her head. "I can't pick out one of these," she whispered, not even daring to look at the sales associate.

"Yes, you can," Russ replied, placing his hand on his hip. Because he wasn't sure of her taste in diamonds, he didn't know which one appealed to her. It would be best if she picked out her own. "Go ahead and choose," he encouraged.

"No." Lynn drew in a deep breath, then with forced courage, she looked at him again. "This isn't right," she insisted in a whisper, hoping the woman assisting them hadn't heard her. Blood rushed through her veins, and the pressure inside her ears increased, blocking out everything around her. An engagement ring signified love and devotion, a promise of forever. Although like many other women she hoped that someday she'd wear the ring of a man who truly loved her, she didn't feel right taking a ring from Russ.

He didn't love her.

And she wasn't in love with him. Not at all, she told herself. Her silent denial of her feelings for him contradicted the sudden pounding of her heart. He took her hand and lifted it, and Lynn tried to pull it back.

"Russ," she pleaded. But she could see in his eyes that his mind was made up.

"It's okay, honey," he told her, drawing her closer. "I'll help. I like this one." He pointed to a princess-cut stone set in gold, graced with smaller triangular diamonds at its sides.

Lynn lost her breath. "That's much too big," she replied quickly. And would cost a fortune—money she was sure Russ didn't have or surely didn't want to spend on her. She stared at the choices, her heart hammering. She didn't want to go through with this, but she wasn't about to embarrass them both in front of the sales associate. "I...uh...they all look so expensive," she said in a low voice.

With a frustrated sigh, he tried again. "Okay, how about this one?" he suggested and picked up another ring, this one cut in the shape of an oval.

"Um, no, I don't think so."

"Okay, let's try this from another angle," Russ suggested, frowning as he picked up a diamond that reminded him of a football. "Try this on," he ordered. Lynn hesitated, and he drew her hand closer. She smacked his hand away, then put it on herself, fussing under her breath.

"There. Are you satisfied? It's too big." She spread her fingers wide so he could see.

"Oh, if you like it, we can have it sized for you," the sales associate quickly assured her.

Lynn immediately took the ring off and put it back in its place. "No, thank you." She hesitantly fingered a couple of other rings, smaller stones that didn't look like they cost more money than a prize race horse. She tried two of them on—one was too small, the other too big.

Russ picked up a round-shaped diamond with a prong setting in a shiny gold band.

"Although we sell many different shapes, that's the most popular," the sales associate assured him. "Do you prefer gold or platinum?" she asked Lynn.

Lynn shrugged, hesitant to reveal her thoughts. "I've never really thought about it."

"Well, you should, dear. You'll be wearing this ring for a long time."

The woman's words hit a nerve, and Lynn grimaced. This engagement ring also signified control—something she'd been trying to get away from. She didn't want to be under Russ's control anymore than she wanted to be under Jake's.

"Try it on," Russ suggested. Before she could stop him, he had her hand in his and was sliding the ring on her finger, slipping it over her knuckle. "It fits," he commented thoughtfully, then looked at Lynn's face. Her expression was hesitant and unsure, but her eyes widened, indicating that she liked the ring.

"It's beautiful, but—"

"Could you excuse us a minute?" Russ said, speaking to the woman helping them. She nodded, putting the display of rings back inside the counter. Then she stepped away, staying close enough to keep an eye on them, but far enough to afford them some privacy.

Russ's gaze met Lynn's as he took both of her hands in his and faced her. Apprehension flashed in her eyes as she looked up at him, followed quickly by surprise and a little bit of wonder as she watched his expression turn serious.

"If this was real, if you were marrying someone you loved and wanted to spend a lifetime with, would you want this ring?" he asked, his tone dropping to a whisper.

"Oh, Russ, what woman wouldn't want a ring this beautiful?" Lynn asked, staring at the brilliant diamond with open appreciation.

"Would *you*, Lynn?" he asked again, his face unreadable.

Lynn gazed at him, and her breath caught. As he pressed closer, butterflies flitted in her stomach. *This isn't real.* "I...yes," she answered honestly, his gaze holding hers. For a moment, they just stared at each other, neither of them speaking. The bold, reassuring look in his eyes made her knees go weak.

She gazed at the ring. Lynn had felt a rush of pleasure when he'd slipped it on her finger, and her entire body still tingled. Her lungs felt starved for air. It was ridiculous, she knew, because she didn't want to get married, but at that moment their engagement felt real, and despite her protests about getting a ring, it felt so right on her, like it belonged there.

That scared her.

Looking back at Russ, she realized he was watching her. His touch was doing crazy things to her insides, making her think about things that weren't possible. Making her want him to kiss her. As if reading her mind, he dipped his head, and she tilted hers in response. Her tongue slipped out and wet her lips. Just as his mouth was about to touch hers, he stopped, and she could feel his entire body stiffen.

"I don't guess we'd better go there," he said, pulling back, his tone serious.

"Um, no. No, we shouldn't," she whispered, and a let-down feeling consumed her. He was right. She knew it. The problem was, her body didn't. She knew she should move out of his arms, but she couldn't.

Suddenly, as if he'd read her thoughts, he let her go, and taking a deep breath, he turned away. He motioned for the woman who'd been helping them to return. "We'll take this one," he said, his tone rough as he spoke. "And the wedding band to match."

"That's a splendid choice," she commented. "If you'll take it off, I'll remove the tag for you."

Lynn started to reach for the ring but was stopped when Russ quickly grasped her hand again. "You don't need to take it off," he told her. It had been hard enough getting her to put on the ring. He wasn't taking any chances on her changing her mind. Turning her hand over, he looked at the woman and said, "You can get the tag off with the ring on her finger, right?"

"Of course, sir," she answered, looking a little confused. She carefully pushed the tiny tag through the gold string, then pulled it free. "I'll just write this up for you."

"Wait here. Don't move," Russ told Lynn. He hesitated until she nodded, then he walked away, following the woman to the register. A few minutes later he was back and they were leaving the mall.

Though Russ walked close beside her as they returned to the truck, he didn't touch her. He couldn't. Touching her made him want her, and he knew Lynn wasn't his to have. She'd made that clear enough. She hadn't wanted his ring. She didn't want him. Sexual chemistry was all there was between them, and if he kept his distance, he could keep that under control.

He should have been feeling relieved instead of agitated. The trouble was he hadn't expected to feel anything when he'd put his ring on her finger. He'd gone through the same ritual with his first wife, and thought his divorce had pretty much settled his feelings on marriage. But something was different about Lynn wearing his ring. She represented everything that he'd once wanted from life—everything he had since come to realize would never be his.

The ring didn't change anything. He had to remember that, as well as he had to remember that he couldn't go around thinking with his libido and not his brain. He'd almost kissed her back there at the jewelry store.

He'd wanted to, he couldn't deny it. As they walked across the parking lot, all he could think about was wanting to do a lot more than kiss her. She stirred all kinds of wants up inside him, and he was having a hard time separating those wants from reality.

He opened her door for her, then got in the driver's side and started the engine. The silence between them was almost palpable. After they were down the road a bit, he chanced a glance at her. Her shoulders were stiff, her posture reserved. Taking a deep breath, he broke the silence between them and asked if she'd like to stop and get some lunch on the way back. He knew it was foolish, but he wanted to be in her company just a little longer.

Lynn shrugged her shoulders. "Sure, if you want," she replied, avoiding looking at him.

He nodded as he turned the truck onto the interstate. They rode in silence until he pulled up to stop at Kelly's, the only diner in Crockett. The restaurant was in an old building, located near the post office, a favorite meeting place for the locals. The place was bustling, and Russ was glad. They would probably run into someone they knew. If they did, it would serve to cut the tension between them.

She didn't wait for him to open her door, but got out and walked beside him to the door of the diner. As he held it open, she stepped inside, careful not to touch him. Because of the plate glass windows across the front, the place was bright and sunny despite black tables and matching chrome and vinyl chairs. They looked almost striking against the white walls.

Russ put his hand at Lynn's back and steered her across the black and white checkered floor toward a booth in the back. They stopped along the way and spoke to several of their neighbors and some of their acquaintances from town. Their waitress approached as they took a seat in the booth.

"Well, hi there, Russ, Lynn. How've you been?" Rebecca Baker asked, placing napkins and silverware in front of them. Handing each of them a menu, she grinned.

Doing her best to return Rebecca's smile, Lynn sat back in her seat. They'd attended school together, but hadn't seen much of each other since graduation. "Fine," she replied, then asked, "How about you?" Realizing that the engagement ring was sitting prominently on her finger, she quickly tucked her hands under the table.

"Oh, pretty good, I guess. Heard you decided not to go to college. You been working out at the ranch?"

Lynn nodded. "Yeah. It keeps me pretty busy."

Rebecca winked, and her gaze slid slowly over Russ. "Doesn't look like that's all that's kept you busy," she commented with a meaningful look.

Lynn's mouth fell open. Before she could speak, Russ leaned forward and pointed at the menu, giving Rebecca his order for lunch.

"I'd like some iced tea with that, please." He didn't miss the way Lynn went to great lengths to hide her engagement ring, like she was ashamed of it, ashamed of him.

Rebecca scribbled on the pad in her hand. "How about you, Lynn?"

"Um, I'll have the same," she replied quickly, just wanting to get rid of her friend. Seeing a high school friend and discussing college made her uncomfortable. She hated any reminder that made her look young in Russ's eyes.

The waitress walked away, and Lynn sucked in a deep breath. "She couldn't possibly know," she stated, alluding to Rebecca's innuendo. "There's no way." She wasn't sure who she was trying to reassure, herself or Russ.

"Anything's possible," Russ told her, his tone gruff. "News spreads quickly, rumors twice as fast."

Lynn shook her head and whispered, "No one in here knows. If they did, if they had any idea we're engaged, they would have mentioned it. I think Rebecca was just guessing."

"Could be," he agreed, wondering himself.

The waitress returned a few minutes later with their order. Because the diner was getting busier, she didn't stop to chat this time, and Lynn was relieved. She and Russ ate their burgers and fries mostly in silence, though they did talk about the work waiting back at the ranch. As Lynn finished eating, she looked around for Rebecca, impatient for their bill so they could leave.

So far it appeared as if word hadn't reached anyone in town. Thank heavens! Maybe this whole pretend engagement wasn't even necessary, Lynn thought. If she was lucky, only her family would think the engagement was real, and it would stay that way. The entire episode could be over before they knew it.

Rebecca came up to their table after a few more minutes had passed. "Is there anything else ya'll need?" she asked. When they both shook their heads, she tore off a page of her tablet and put it on the table. Then she gasped, ''Oh my, Lynn McCall! Look at that diamond on your hand!'' Her astonished gaze flitted back and forth between Lynn and Russ. Then, as if a lightbulb came on inside her head, she exclaimed in a voice loud enough to still the entire diner, ''You're engaged!''

Five

Lynn blushed to the roots of her blond hair as heads in the diner swivelled in their direction, then she broke out in a sweat as everyone in the place started clapping. Hoots and whistles followed. Feeling a lot like a bird trapped by a cat, she shrank down in her seat. It was all she could do not to bend her head and hide her face. Her hand started to shake and she nearly knocked over her glass of iced tea, catching it just before it toppled.

Everyone in the diner was looking at them. Some of the people were getting out of their seats and coming toward them. She looked to Russ, panic in her eyes.

"Do something!" she hissed, then, with a frozen smile on her lips, faced Rebecca who had grabbed Lynn's hand to inspect the ring she'd received from Russ only a short while ago. The waitress squealed again when she got a closer look at it. The diamond sparkled, twinkling as the woman tilted Lynn's hand back and forth.

"Like what?" Russ wasn't sure what she wanted him to do. He'd told her that word would get out. He figured they might as well face it now. Besides, he wasn't any happier than she was about the commotion. He was used to keeping his distance from people, not sharing his thoughts or being the center of attention.

His voice was smothered by the chatter of the group gathering around their table. Although he'd known these people only a few years, Lynn had known them her entire life. It wasn't unusual for her friends and neighbors to be interested in her or for news of her engagement to be something to talk about.

Larry Melton, the owner of the feed store in Crockett, slapped Russ on the back good-naturedly. "You lucky dog!" he declared, wriggling his eyebrows with a silly grin on his face.

Fixing a smile on his face, Russ replied, his voice a little unsteady, "That I am." He glanced again at Lynn, who looked about to be smothered by the throng of women trying to get a closer look at her ring. Mrs. Weaver, known for being the biggest gossip in Crockett, was maneuvering her way through the group gathering at their table. She used her ample body to push those closest to Lynn aside.

"I haven't heard a word about anything goin' on between you two. When did all this happen?" she asked baldly, her keen eyes shifting back and forth between Russ and Lynn.

"Well, we—"

Lynn was saved from answering when Jeannie Bates, the clerk at the small grocery store, stated excitedly, "Boy, you McCalls are all getting hitched!" She took a turn looking at the ring, staring at it with envy. "First Ryder, then Jake and now you!"

"Yeah, what's in the water out there?" Ty Colbert asked Russ, then chuckled. "Think I'll stick to beer!" Ty was Deke's age, and he was well known in Crockett for his love-'em-and-leave-'em reputation.

He groaned when his current girlfriend, Samantha Evans, elbowed him in the ribs. "It wouldn't hurt you to think about marriage," she chided with a look of reproach. "I've been tryin' for months to get him to propose," she said wistfully. She glanced at Lynn as she stared at the ring. "Oh, it is so beautiful!"

Lynn wanted to crawl under the table. She glanced over and shot a get-me-out-of-here look at Russ. He was talking to one of the men, and she kicked his leg under the table to get his attention.

"Ow!" Russ's eyes pinned her with an accusing stare. It wasn't as if this was his fault.

Lynn was smiling, but he could tell from her expression that she wasn't at all happy. Her face was nearly bloodred. He scooted to the edge of his seat, then managed to get out and stand beside the booth. Moving slowly among the well-wishers, he made his way to Lynn, pulling out his wallet and tossing some money on the table to pay for their meal.

He accepted congratulations from nearly everyone before he could get a hold of Lynn's hand and make room for her to get out of her seat. As she stood, he put his arm around her shoulders. The crowd was still talking to them as they slowly made their way to the door.

Russ studied Lynn as she walked beside him, a smile fixed on her pretty face, anxiety in her eyes. Her face was still flushed, her skin hot. He knew how she felt. He'd never admit it to her, but he'd been unable to get a steady breath since they'd left the jewelry store, and all the attention and hoopla wasn't helping.

"Have you set a date?" someone asked as they reached the door.

"No, we haven't," Lynn said quickly as Russ held the door for her. "We haven't made any definite plans." She rushed out without saying another word. Turning, she glanced back as Russ grabbed her hand. People were still calling congratulations to them through the open door as they walked toward his truck. He held the passenger door for her, then joined her, going around the truck and getting into the driver's seat.

"I can't believe that just happened." Lynn tried to get her bearings, her breathing uneven.

"Not much goes on around here. People get excited when they hear good news."

"Good news?" she repeated, sounding offended. Her voice rose. "This isn't good news!" she declared. "It isn't even real."

Russ's jaw tightened as he headed away from Crockett toward the Bar M. Every time she said it like that, his gut began to churn. She made it sound like marriage to him would be the worse thing that could happen to her. Well, he had news for her, it wasn't. She could turn up pregnant and not married. In today's culture, maybe that wasn't frowned on so much. But here in the county of Crockett, it was something to talk about.

He'd been laughed at in Montana when Candace had turned up pregnant by another man. He'd be damned if he was going to wind up looking like a fool again. "It's a reality you're gonna have to face. You could be pregnant," he reminded her, his tone agitated.

Lynn glared at him, drawing her brows together. "I...am...not...pregnant!"

Russ's expression hardened a fraction as he glanced in her direction. "You don't know that." She sure was determined not to be pregnant with his child. Well, he should have expected that. She was letting him know again that the night they spent together meant nothing to her. He should have been relieved.

But he wasn't.

His gaze traveled over her, and his gut twisted. His attention shifted to her trim thighs, and desire slammed him. How could he want her so badly? He couldn't remember a time when a woman affected him to the point of distraction. Though he'd been married to Candace, he'd never been aroused this easily by her.

"Though someday I do want a family," Lynn admitted, "it just isn't in my immediate plans." She picked that moment to turn her head in Russ's direction. His hardened expression gave her cause for thought. He didn't seem any happier than she was about their circumstances.

A knot formed in her throat. He'd been attentive and loving with her last night, showing her a side of himself that she'd never seen. That he would readily give up his freedom for her proved he was a man of honor. Even as he glowered at her, she admired that about him.

She was surprised that he hadn't been snapped up by a woman by now. Considering he was a loner and somewhat unapproachable, despite his attractive looks, women probably thought twice about approaching him unless he spoke first.

"Things don't always go as planned," Russ reminded her. They sure hadn't last night. He'd never *planned* on taking her to bed.

"You're right about that," she answered. "I never counted on this complication." Never in her life would she have thought she'd have to consider Russ in her plans. Before last night, she could have staked her life on the fact that she never would have so much as kissed him, let alone given him her innocence.

"Darn it!" she squealed, and her hands balled into fists.

"What?" Her outburst startled Russ, and he slammed his foot on the brake pedal, pitching them both forward. Their seat belts prevented them from being thrown into the dashboard.

Lynn turned in her seat to face him. "We could have settled whether I was pregnant or not easily enough with a home pregnancy test!" she exclaimed. "Supposedly, you can tell within minutes if you're pregnant."

Russ nodded. Even though he was still planning to marry her, it would be nice to know if pregnancy was a factor. "Do you want to turn around?" he asked.

"And buy one in Crockett? Good heavens, no!" She straightened and settled more comfortably in her seat. "Can you imagine walking into Walker's Grocery and buying a pregnancy test? Do you want everyone in the county to know I could be pregnant?"

Walker's was the small local store with a pharmacy

in the back that everyone in Crockett frequented. It also was a meeting place for some of the older folks to pass the day. "I see what you mean."

She sighed deeply. "We should have picked one up while we were in San Luis. No one there would have known us."

Russ pushed the gas pedal and slowly started the truck moving again. "Do you want to go back to San Luis now?" he asked, glancing at his watch. It was afternoon, and they really needed to get back to the ranch.

"We don't have time. There's a lot to do this afternoon," she said, thinking they'd have to work hard and fast just to get everything done before sunset.

"Yeah," Russ agreed as they approached the wood-and-iron sign stating they were on McCall land. He turned the truck onto a side road and continued up the hillside leading to the main house.

"We'll just have to get one as soon as possible. Maybe I can get away in a couple of days," she said as they passed over a small ridge. They drove by the narrow airstrip and hangar designed for the Cessna plane that Jake and Catherine had taken when they'd left for their honeymoon.

Russ steered the truck behind his quarters and stopped it, letting the engine idle to keep the air-conditioning going. "I guess we'd better get to work," he commented, realizing that he wasn't really anxious to be relieved of Lynn's company.

Lynn favored him with a look that told him she had other plans. "You don't think I'm gonna walk into the house by myself, do you?" she demanded.

Shrugging and looking confused, Russ replied, "What are you talkin' about?"

Lynn exhaled, and her bangs flew upward. "This ring is what I'm talking about," she informed him, shaking her hand in his face. Her voice sounded cynical.

Russ stared at her. When she didn't go on, he prompted, "What about it?"

"Men!" Lynn huffed, and opened her door. She got out as Russ killed the engine and joined her.

Looking at a loss, Russ stared at her, his face blank. "What?"

"Oh, just forget it." She walked away from him, muttering something under her breath about the male gender and their lack of intelligence.

"Wait a minute!" Russ called, catching her by the arm and pulling her around to face him. Her momentum carried her into his embrace. He slipped his arms around her and held her so she couldn't move. "What are you trying to say?" he asked, sounding dumbfounded.

"Never mind," she replied not looking at him, stubbornly refusing to enlighten him. "Let me go."

"Not yet," he told her, though he was thinking that was exactly what he should do. He needed to let her go before he did something stupid—like kiss her. Feeling her against him, smelling her, made him want to do more than hold her. Russ worked to get his thoughts under control. "What's the problem?"

Taking a deep breath, Lynn lifted her face to his. "Do you know what's going to happen when I walk in that door?"

Russ shook his head.

"Ashley's going to be all over me, fussing over the ring and this whole engagement mess." She didn't want to contend with her sister-in-law's excitement alone. Thank goodness Catherine's younger sister, Bethany, had already left, as well. That was one less person she'd have to face.

"Oh."

"Yeah, oh."

"You're right. I should have thought about it. We're in this together so I'll go up to the house with you," he told her. He let her go, but took her hand. "C'mon."

Lynn tried to pull away from him as they started toward the house, but he tightened his hold. Crossing the dusty yard, they headed for the house.

Ashley met them as they came in the door. Her face lit with excitement, and she rushed toward them. Lynn didn't even try to pretend why. She was getting good at this pretending thing. Fixing a smile on her face wide enough to show her straight white teeth, she lifted her hand and showed her sister-in-law the ring.

"Oh, it's beautiful!" Ashley hugged them both, her eyes bright with enthusiasm.

As she continued to fuss over the ring, Lynn tried to move away from Russ, but he put his arm around her, playing the part of her fiancé, making it seem all too real.

"I'm just so happy for you!" Ashley exclaimed, oblivious of the tension between Lynn and Russ.

"Thank you," Lynn said, trying her best to sound as if she meant it. She darted a look at Russ. She resented that he looked relaxed when she felt as if someone had a gun in her back.

"Well, now you're gonna have to start thinking about a date."

Lynn and Russ stared at each other. "We're discussing it," Russ said quickly, not giving Lynn a chance to speak.

"Great! Just don't take too long. A wedding takes a while to plan." She smiled brightly at Lynn. "I know you'll want it to be perfect."

Lynn nodded and gave Ashley the happy smile she was expecting. "Um, I've got a couple of things to do," she said, turning toward Russ with a look of pure distress. "I'll be out in a few minutes."

"Sure." Russ was aware of Ashley watching them. Thinking it would look odd if he just walked away from Lynn, he thought he'd better kiss her to keep up the pretense. Even as he made the decision, he was anxious for the taste of her. "I'll see you in a few minutes," he told her, lowering his head and pulling her closer.

Caught off guard, Lynn looked startled when she realized his intention. But with Ashley watching them, she had no choice but to lift her lips to Russ's and accept his kiss. As his mouth descended, her breath caught with anticipation.

Expecting a brief touching of their lips, Lynn wasn't prepared when Russ slid his hand behind her neck and held her still as their mouths met. Her hands went to his chest and rested there, trembling slightly. The pressure of his hand might have brought her to him, but the desire to be kissed by him kept her there, made her ache for more.

Before she knew it, he was stepping away and letting her go. Lynn struggled for her balance, and as if sensing her need for help, Russ rested his hand behind her back, then intimately caressed her before he moved away. Without another word, he turned and walked out.

* * *

He was losing his mind.

Russ removed the saddle from the horse he'd been working with and carried it into the barn. He'd recently purchased the horse with the idea of starting his own livestock. While normally the horses he worked with grazed in a pasture, Russ wanted to keep this one in a stall for a few days. Surrounded by the acrid odor of hay and manure, he shouldn't have been cognizant of Lynn's scent, but he smelled her the moment she followed him into the barn and led the horse to a stall.

It had been a hectic, yet strange week. He watched her as she removed the halter from the horse and stepped back to close the latch. Russ was becoming attuned to her every mood—the way she became animated and excited when something pleased her, the way her brows dipped into a soft frown when she was concentrating, her quiet manner when something was bothering her.

Like now.

She'd said little to him all morning. Not that they'd engaged in much more than necessary conversation since the day they'd gone to pick out the ring. Knowing that they'd draw suspicion from Ashley and Ryder if they didn't appear to be getting along, Russ figured he'd better see what was bothering her.

"Something wrong?" he asked, watching her.

She shrugged, then gave the horse a stroke on the bridge of his nose.

Russ walked over to her and touched her shoulder. She stepped away from him as if she didn't want his hands on her. His lips twisting with irritation, he pinned her against the stall with his hands on either side of her on the railing.

"Maybe you'd better tell me what's botherin' you," he said, annoyed by her distant demeanor. She was driving him crazy! It had been a week since he'd touched her, and he found working with her tested his will to keep his hands off of her. Dipping his head, he forced her to look at him.

"I'm just tired," she answered evasively. Lynn knew it sounded more like an excuse than the truth. She hoped Russ didn't push her. Even though they'd been intimate and she'd told him about wanting to start her own horse farm, she wasn't really used to sharing her thoughts with him. The past few days between them had been tense, both of them keeping to their own company as much as possible without causing suspicion. Her desire to remain distant seemed at war with a part of her that wanted to feel his mouth on hers again.

"It's more than that," Russ said knowingly, stepping closer.

Lynn lifted her face and stared into his eyes. "It's been a busy week, that's all," she insisted, finding it hard to breathe with him so near. She chewed on her lip with her teeth. When she realized he wasn't going to give up, she felt heat rise to her cheeks. "Okay. I haven't had a chance to get to San Luis. I wanted to get that…um…you know."

"Yeah, I know," he admitted, and he was just as frustrated. It had been on his mind, too. It was one thing to sleep with her, to steal her innocence. Though Ryder had accepted it when Russ had promised he'd marry Lynn, he wasn't sure what her brother would have to say if his little sister turned up pregnant.

"Look, it'll be okay. I'm planning to go into San Luis tomorrow afternoon with Ryder to meet a client. Maybe I can get one while I'm there."

Lynn stared directly at him, and her mouth dropped open. "You're kidding." Her lips quirked up into a smile. "*You're* gonna buy one and bring it back?"

Nodding, Russ tried to keep his own lips from twitching. This had to be the most obscure conversation he'd ever had. "Well, I'm not exactly excited about the idea, but I think I can get the chore done." His gaze traveled to her mouth, then again to her baby blue eyes. "You're gonna have to give me an idea of what to look for though. It's not like I've done it before."

Lynn tucked that piece of information away in her mind as she lifted her foot and propped the heel of her boot against the stall. "You shouldn't have any trouble. It's not hard to figure out. It should be in the pharmacy section of any big discount store. If you go into a drugstore, though, look around in the area for birth control." Catching a vivid mental picture of Russ roaming the aisles looking for a pregnancy test, she chuckled. "But I'm wondering, how are you gonna accomplish that task with Ryder along?"

Russ shook his head. "Damned if I know," he admitted, watching her tongue as it slipped out of her mouth and licked her lip. He felt the bottom half of his body stir. He wondered if she had any idea of what that did to him. If she kept it up, he was gonna have to taste her.

Ryder walked in at that moment, followed by a tabby cat that scampered behind a bale of hay. Russ turned toward him, his movement bringing his body into contact with Lynn's. When she started to move away, he put his hand on her hip, keeping her next to him.

Grinning, Ryder winked at them from across the barn as he disappeared into the tack room. He came out with some gauze pads and some antibiotic ointment. "You two aren't gonna get any work done like that," he told them, a big grin on his face.

"We were just talking," Lynn retorted, aware that her body felt as if it was on fire. Though she wanted to move away from Russ, her feet just weren't obeying. His heat seeped into her, stirring her awareness of him. Without thinking about it, she lifted her hand and placed it along his stomach. The muscles in his abdomen tightened in response to the intimate gesture, and the awareness between them intensified.

"Yeah, right. Ashley and I talk just like that sometimes," Ryder quipped, clearly amused at catching them in an intimate embrace. He strolled out of the barn whistling.

Still holding Lynn next to him, Russ turned toward her. The barn fell silent except for the occasional stirring of the horses. Despite his promise to himself to keep his desire for Lynn in check, Russ felt his self-control slipping. Her mouth was so damn tempting.

To hell with his promise to himself, he decided, feeling reckless. What could one kiss hurt? His heart was still under lock and key. As long as he let it end with a kiss...

Raising his hand, he cupped Lynn's face and lifted it. Before she had a chance to protest, which he didn't want to give her, he swooped down and claimed her lips. They were soft and warm and, hell, everything he remembered. An ache stirred in his chest, then slowly traveled lower to his belly. When she didn't pull away, he slipped his arms around her, bringing her more into his embrace. She felt delicate and soft, all woman.

He groaned his satisfaction as she moved her hand over his ribs, sliding it around his side, aligning her body with his. Her breasts grazed his chest, fueling his desire to have more of her. He darted his tongue into her mouth, urging her to open for him, to give him full access to her depths. She made a tiny sound of pleasure in her throat, and that was all it took for him to seek more, demand more.

As she opened her mouth, he deepened the kiss and groaned with satisfaction as his tongue found hers. His hand slid from her back to her waist, then languidly up her rib cage and hovered near her breast. As if hungering for his touch, she arched toward him, pressing closer, moving against him, encouraging him.

His hips pinned her against the stall door, and she lifted her leg. Russ gathered her closer, his hands going to her bottom and lifting her firmly against him, their clothing a barrier that added friction to their passion.

He groaned again as her palms caressed his back, then moved lower to his hips, then lower still, and she pulled him against her.

Knowing he couldn't take her was painful agony. Forgetting where they were, he sought the snap of her jeans. Tugging at it, it popped open, and he slid his hands inside and cupped her buttocks. Her skin was like warm silk. Just touching her made his blood race in his veins.

"Easy, honey," he said, knowing he needed to stop himself before things got any more out of control.

His voice caused her to open her eyes, and her haze cleared almost instantly. She tried to push away from him, her breathing ragged. Russ went still, wishing the moment didn't have to end. He wanted her more now than ever.

"Damn," he whispered. "I shouldn't have let things get out of hand. I'm sorry." Hearing voices in the distance, he quickly set her away from him. "Better get yourself together," he told her quickly, then turned away, blocking her from view as she straightened her clothing. After a moment, she moved around him and looked at him. Her cheeks were warm and rosy. His gaze slid down her body, then traveled back to her face.

"It's okay," he told her, sucking in a hard breath. But *he* wasn't. He was aching, hurting for her. He started to touch her again, but stopped himself as one of the hands joined them in the barn.

Hell.

Six

Lynn glanced out the window of the ranch office just in time to see the black pickup come to a complete stop near the bunkhouse. Her heart skipped a beat. Russ was back from San Luis! She hadn't seen him since their encounter in the barn yesterday. Her face grew hot just thinking about the way she'd come apart in his arms. What was happening to her? She didn't want or need this complication in her life. Aware that she had little choice but to admit to herself that her emotions were increasingly at risk where Russ was concerned, Lynn trembled.

Her physical attraction to him was going to be difficult to control if she wasn't careful. Was it even possible for her to continue being near him without wanting him to make love to her? He'd shown a heck of a lot more willpower yesterday than she had, that was for sure. Or maybe it wasn't willpower. Maybe he didn't really want her, and he'd just been amusing himself. He hadn't even tried to take what had happened between them to completion.

She watched as Ryder and Russ got out of the truck. They stood for a few minutes talking, then parted company. Her heartbeat quickened as she watched Russ unload some things from the back of the pickup, then he disappeared inside his quarters.

Had he had a chance to get the pregnancy test? Lynn couldn't tell a thing from the bags that he'd carried in, but, oh, she hoped so. She wanted the issue of pregnancy settled. Then she and Russ could figure a way to get out of their pretend engagement.

The sooner that was solved, the sooner she could begin to distance herself from him. Despite his abrupt manner and his obstinate opinion of how their problem should be handled, she was actually starting to *like* him.

And that scared her to death.

She didn't want to like Russ. And she didn't want to be attracted to him. She looked down at her hand, graced by the beautiful ring Russ had bought her. Though she knew in her heart it was for nothing more than show, a tiny, feminine part of her wondered what it would feel like if it stood for something more.

Russ Logan, she was learning, was an incredible man with many facets to his personality. Once his mind was made up, he stood by his decisions. He was also honorable and protective, putting her well-being ahead of his own.

Unable to stand waiting to find out if he'd had a chance to pick up the pregnancy test, she decided to go and ask him. Just as she was about to look away, she saw Russ come back outside and walk into the barn. Thinking she'd catch up with him, she rushed from the room, nearly bumping into her pregnant sister-in-law.

"Oops, sorry, Ashley. Are you all right?" Lynn asked, stepping around her.

Ashley looked at her curiously. "Yes, but where are you headed in such a hurry?"

"Um, just outside." She avoided Ashley's direct gaze, focusing instead on her swollen belly.

"Oh. Well, do you have a few minutes? I was wondering if you and Russ had settled on a date for the wedding yet. It's been over a week since we found out about you two, and you haven't said a word."

She didn't have to say that it wasn't normally in Lynn's character to keep to her own confidence. Lynn was well-known for being an extrovert. Around the McCall household, it was a rare occurrence when she *didn't* speak her mind. "Actually no, we haven't settled that." Lynn stopped herself from divulging more information than she wanted.

"But you've talked about it, right?" Ashley pressed.

"A little." Lynn crossed her fingers behind her back, and she edged a tiny bit closer to the door.

Ashley looked at her with speculation. "Do you have a time frame of some kind?"

Put on the spot, Lynn couldn't even think straight. "Six months," she declared, thinking that was a plausible amount of time. That would give her and Russ a reasonable amount of time to break off their engagement.

"Jeez," Ashley gasped. "That's hardly enough time to plan a proper wedding, especially with the baby arriving." She put her palm against her stomach and patted it. "Do you want me to start making some preliminary notes?"

"Um, yeah, sure," Lynn replied, distracted. "Right now I have something to do. Can we talk about this later?" She barely waited for Ashley's response before she took off and went out the front door.

Whew, that was close. She walked across the yard toward the barn. She was almost there when she spotted Russ. He'd already saddled a palomino stallion and was working with him inside the corral. The horse was almost ready to be returned to his owner.

She climbed up on the fence and leaned her elbows over the top to hold herself in position. Watching him, she realized how fortunate she'd been to work with him all these months. Though he hadn't allowed her to move as fast in training as she'd hoped, he'd been a good mentor. A year of working with him had taught her that, she reluctantly admitted. While earlier she'd complained to Jake that Russ was dragging his feet training her, as she watched him with the horse, she was awed by his remarkable patience and skill and realized how very lucky she was to work with him.

If he hadn't been so ornery most of the time, they would've argued less and she might even have *enjoyed* working with him.

A little while later, he dismounted and started loosening the saddle, then hefted it on his shoulder and walked toward the gate. Watching the byplay of the muscles in his arms and chest, Lynn gulped, then realized she'd been caught staring when he stopped at the gate and looked up at her. Without speaking, she jumped off the fence as he opened the gate. Avoiding his gaze, she closed it for him. However it wasn't possible to ignore his intense look, and she felt compelled to face him.

"I was wondering if you had a chance to take care of that errand we talked about?" Lynn was beginning to hate the blush that rose to her cheeks whenever she broached the subject of the pregnancy test.

Russ nodded. He'd noticed her coming across the yard and had already figured out what she wanted. She'd pretty much avoided him after their intimate interlude in the barn, and he'd been wondering if he was going to have to go and find her. "It wasn't easy, but, yeah, I did actually."

He started walking toward the barn, and she fell into step beside him, careful not to get too close. She actually had to stop herself from touching him. "If you give it to me, I can, um, take care of it."

"It's in my room," he informed her, walking inside and dumping the saddle in the barn. He turned and looked at her. "I'll get it for you."

Nodding, ready to get it over with, she followed him to his quarters. Russ reached his door, opened it and stood back for her to enter. Lynn flashed him a quick glance, then stepped inside. Immediately upon entering, her entire body felt as if it had gone through a time warp. Her gaze went to the unmade bed, and she saw an image of herself there, naked and writhing against him. A knot formed in her throat, and she swallowed hard to dislodge it.

As if unaware of her dilemma, Russ disappeared into the bathroom. To keep her mind busy, she glanced around the room. Other than the bed, everything was basically tidy, with only a few things out of place. He'd been reading, she noticed, as she picked up a mystery novel on his bedside table. It was a popular title, written by a well-known writer. A torn piece of newspaper inserted a quarter of the way through served as a bookmark.

Digesting that, she put it down. She didn't know Russ liked to read. Actually, she really didn't know a lot about him personally, and she realized that regardless of what happened between them, she was curious about him.

She swung around when she heard a noise. Russ had walked back into the room and had a small brown bag in his hand.

"This wasn't the easiest thing in the world to get. There was a lot of stuff to choose from." As she approached him, Russ was distracted by the gentle sway of her breasts.

"Let me see." He held it out to her, and she opened the bag and took out a blue box with black writing.

"How does it work?"

Frowning, she put her hand on her hip. Her gaze came up to meet his. "I really wouldn't know."

Russ took a step back. She was close enough for him to touch, and he was having trouble resisting the temptation. He hadn't been able to think straight since yesterday when he'd kissed her in the barn. "I was just asking. I figured since you're a woman, you'd know about these things."

Lynn sank down on the edge of his bed. "Ah, like it's something every woman should know about? Kinda like all men should know the year and make of a car just by looking at it?"

Russ dignified her words with a nod. "Well, yeah." He sat beside her on the bed. It dipped with his weight, shifting her closer to him, and the sweet scent of her reached his nostrils.

She made a face at him, and he grinned. Then she became conscious of how close they were sitting and tried to scoot away a little as she returned her attention to the box and studied it. "This doesn't look right," she said, ignoring the quickening of her pulse. She held it a little closer. "I don't think you bought the right thing." Concentrating again on the box, she was quiet for a moment.

Before she realized his intention, Russ took the box from her. "It has the word pregnancy right there on it," he pointed out, stabbing at it with his index finger. Lynn grabbed at the box, but he held it out of her reach, using his other arm to ward off her attempts at getting it back.

"Russ, give me that!" she demanded, and her voice rose. She caught him off guard and snatched it from him, then studied the box again. "You idiot! This isn't a pregnancy test," she wailed. "It's a kit to determine ovulation!"

He'd been grappling with her, shoving the kit away from where she had it prominently displayed in front of his face. His movements suddenly stopped. "What?"

"You know, the kind of test a woman takes when she *wants* to get pregnant." Her tone was less than tolerant. "How on earth did you pick this up by mistake?" she asked sharply, getting to her feet, her stance rigid.

"I told you there was a lot of stuff to choose from," he said, defending himself, charging to his feet to confront her. "You were the one who said it wouldn't be hard."

"Well, you were the one who said you'd get it. If I'd known you couldn't do it right, I'd have found a way to do it myself."

"I did the best I could under the circumstances! Or did you want your brother to know what I was buying? As it was, I had to make up an excuse to leave the meeting and sneak into a nearby store to hunt for the damn thing!"

Lynn glared at him. "Well, you couldn't have gotten it more wrong!"

Russ grabbed the box from her and threw it at the trash can. It bounced off the rim, then fell inside. "We'll get another one, then."

"I don't know when." They were both aware that fall was a busy time on the ranch. Everyone was expected to pitch in and help get the work done and that included both of them.

"Hell, we'll just have to make time," he stated, glaring at her, annoyed that they'd have to wait. He took a deep breath and was quiet for a moment. "Look," he told her, making an obvious effort to talk in a civil tone, "it won't do any good to argue about it. There's nothing we can do until we get one."

"I know," she answered, her tone more rational as she calmed down. Still, disappointment shadowed her eyes.

Russ stared at her, then he moved closer to her and put his hand on her shoulder. "I'm really sorry I messed it up."

Lynn focused on the strong column of his throat. His nearness was causing havoc inside her. It had been in this very room that he'd made love to her. Unable to speak, she lifted her gaze, and his green eyes drew hers. She touched his chest, laying her palm against it, and she felt his body tense. "I'm sorry, too, for yelling at you. It's really not your fault." For a moment, they stared at each other in crushing silence.

"Damn." Russ had been in control until she'd touched him. All hell broke loose inside him, and he reached for her, pulling her tight against him. "You're going to be the death of me yet," he whispered, sounding frustrated. Then he brought his mouth down hard on hers.

Lips touched, tongues met. Their bodies melded together as passion exploded between them. His hands were at her blouse almost immediately, jerking it from her pants. All Lynn could think about was helping him get it off. She wanted to feel his hands on her body. She'd die if she had to wait a moment longer. As he quickly worked the buttons through the loops, she began to do the same to his shirt. A button popped off. She wasn't sure whose it was, but she didn't really care.

She was down to just her bra and jeans by the time he backed her against the bed, and they fell in a heap on it. His body pressed hard against hers, and she struggled to help him get his shirt off, kissing him back as if her very life depended on it.

"Hurry," she pleaded, her hips writhing as her bra fell away and his hand covered her breast. His thumb grazed her nipple as his mouth found the other one. She arched her back as his teeth gently teased it. Her breath came in snatches. She moaned deep and low in her throat, a wild hunger exploding inside her.

In a frenzy of desire, she felt for his belt and struggled to unbuckle it. Grunting, he sucked his stomach when the back of her hand made contact with his skin.

She ran her hand down the front of his fly, discovering he was hard and ready for her. Then he was kissing her again, deeper, thrusting his tongue into her mouth as he worked her jeans down. He pulled off her boots, then yanked her panties down her thighs. They joined her jeans on the floor.

All the while she was trying to shove his jeans and his dark blue briefs down. He helped her enough to get them out of the way. She opened her legs for him and felt the velvet tip of his shaft intimately touch her. He was pushing inside when he suddenly stilled. His entire body became stiff, and he struggled for a breath.

"Damn."

"Don't stop," she rasped, her body on fire.

"Lynn—"

"Don't. I want you now, Russ. Please." Pulling his head down to her, she kissed him, sliding her tongue into his mouth.

He dragged his mouth from hers. "I have to protect you," he told her, easing away. He leaned over her, and she heard him open a drawer, then heard the tearing of a packet. And then he was with her again, sliding into her, filling her with himself. She felt the impact of his full weight as his hands grabbed her hips and he shoved harder, deeper into the core of her.

"Ah," she rasped, her teeth clenched. Earth-shattering pleasure filled her, and she wrapped her legs around his back and held on. Minutes later, her cry was quickly followed by his, and he collapsed on top of her. Their heavy breathing filled the room.

Russ stirred first, and Lynn felt cool air hit her skin

as he rested himself on his elbows and looked down at her. His gaze was hard, his jaw tight.

"I didn't mean for this to happen."

Blushing furiously, she looked away. "Neither did I," she admitted, her voice raspy. He glared at her then, and she looked away and started to wriggle from beneath him. He moved and sat up, and as gracefully as possible, she scooted to the edge of the bed. Spotting her panties and jeans, she turned her back to Russ as she stood and began dressing, sliding both articles of clothing over her rear and hips in one fluid movement. "Don't make a big deal out of this. Things just got out of hand."

"Yeah, right. We just happened to fall into bed again."

"So we're physically attracted to each other. It doesn't mean anything," she assured him. "Since neither of us wanted this to happen, it won't happen again."

Russ moved off the bed and yanked his clothes in place, his movements agitated and awkward as he made his way to the bathroom. His heart hardened at her dismissal.

When he walked back into the room, she was running her hands through her hair, brushing it from her eyes. His gaze slid over her body, vividly remembering how it felt to be inside her. He looked away and reminded himself that he was playing a dangerous game by becoming more involved with her. Despite the warning, he felt himself harden.

Damn, he wanted her again.

Noticing his rigid stance, Lynn cleared her throat. "At least this time, we used protection." That was only because of his self-control. She'd been begging him to make love to her. Her body felt deliciously satisfied, and she trembled slightly. "I'd better go," she stated, watching him. She wasn't sure what he was thinking, but his dark look didn't encourage conversation.

Russ nodded, but didn't speak. She was awfully eager to be out of his company. He was damned if he was going to apologize for making love to her again. "I'll try to get another test in the next few days. Or maybe we can get away together and pick one up," he suggested.

"In a couple of weeks I'll have my, uh…" she left the words unspoken, but she knew he picked up on her meaning by his expression. "It won't hurt to just wait until then."

"You're sure?" He wasn't convinced it was best to put it off. He'd feel better if he knew before Jake got back from his honeymoon.

"Yes. I'm sure I'm not pregnant. If I'm late it will be because of the anxiety from all that's happened. Let's just wait." It was then that she remembered her conversation with Ashley. As much as she hated to bring it up, she had no choice but to tell Russ that she'd put a deadline on their imaginary nuptials. She stared at her feet, then drew in a deep breath and faced him. "Uh, there's something kind of important that I should probably tell you."

"I'm listening."

"There's a complication that I, well, I didn't mean to, uh…" She stopped talking when she saw the wary look in his eyes. She was hesitant to go on, but forced herself to admit what she'd said. "What I'm trying to say is that I sort of told Ashley that we'd set a time for the wedding.'' She waited with bated breath for his reaction.

Russ's brows lifted. ''You what?''

''She pinned me down, and I didn't know what to tell her.'' As he approached, she inched backward.

''What exactly did you say?'' he demanded, his expression guarded.

''It's not as bad as it sounds,'' she said quickly, reassuring herself more than him.

''Spit it out, Lynn.'' Russ was losing his patience with her. She didn't want a relationship with him, but she sure seemed as eager as he had to make love again. She didn't want to get married, but she'd set a time frame for their wedding. She was confusing the hell out of him.

''All right, all right,'' she answered, glaring at him. ''Ashley was asking me if we'd set a date. I told her no, but she kept talking, going on about how hard it is to plan a wedding. I thought if I just gave in and told her that we'd talked about it, she'd let it go. So you see, I really did us a favor.''

''A favor? You did us a favor?''

''I didn't set a date, really. More like a definite time frame.''

''And that is...'' He waited, and the muscle in his jaw flexed.

''Six months.'' Rather than being upset, he appeared puzzled. She stared at him, wondering what he was thinking.

''Six months?'' he repeated, shaking his head. ''We're not waiting six months to get married.''

''We're *not* getting married.''

''Yes, we are,'' he told her, his tone set, his back rigid. ''But we're not waiting six months. We're not even waiting six weeks.'' Marrying her would cause problems, but he'd never thought once about backing off from his word.

Lynn threw her hands up in frustration. Anger stiffened her spine. Squaring her shoulders, she exclaimed, ''I can't talk to you about this anymore.'' She pushed past him and stomped toward the door.

''Running away won't help,'' Russ shouted back. ''We need to settle this, here and now.''

''I'm not settling this, Russ. No way. I don't want to get married to you. When I get married, it'll be because I'm in love. Having sex with you again hasn't changed anything.''

Russ's gut twisted as her blunt words gouged his heart. He should have been prepared for the pain, but in some indescribable way, it hurt more coming from Lynn. Just like his mother, just like Candace, Lynn didn't want him. ''You can fight it all you want, but it's going to happen. Sooner than you think.''

He wasn't going to change his mind. She'd made it clear that she had relegated what happened between them as lust. He could live with that if she could. He wasn't planning on staying married to her any longer than he had to—just long enough to protect her reputation and to make her brothers happy.

She opened the door and stomped out.

Seven

Russ had thought about it long and hard, and eventually he'd decided to give Lynn a little time to settle down and come around to his way of thinking, but apparently she wasn't planning on surrendering easily. Whether she wanted to admit it or not, she was just as trapped as he was by this whole episode. Annoyed that she was holding her stand against marrying him, he concluded he might have to take a step to push the issue. By the way she was avoiding him, that wasn't going to be easy.

She barely spoke to him, which caused even more friction between them. His gut tightened as he watched her dismount the horse she'd been training. He couldn't seem to take his eyes off the enticing sway of her hips as she moved around the animal.

He couldn't remember a time in his life when he'd wanted a woman this badly. No, not just a woman. It was Lynn he wanted. And though she might want to deny it, she wanted him just as much. But as she'd so bluntly put it, they weren't in love with each other, nor did they want to be. It would be best if he stuck to his original plan and kept his distance from her. He hadn't meant to make love to her again. It had just sort of happened. He'd kissed her and had lost his head. He'd have to be more careful in the future.

Swearing under his breath, he walked over to her and offered some advice on her technique. She listened intently as he spoke, looking him directly in the eyes. He had to hand it to her, she seemed to have more of a grip on her emotions than he did. She absently licked her lips, and Russ felt his chest squeeze.

"You've done a good job with him."

Her head came up and she looked at him, caution in her eyes. "Do you mean that?" He'd never given her much indication of whether he felt she knew what she was doing. In the past, they'd pretty much argued about everything involving her training. She wasn't sure if he was being sincere.

Russ eyed her with open speculation. He sensed that her confidence at this point was fragile, and he supposed that was his fault. He'd held back his encouragement because of Jake. She deserved to know that she was good, deserved to hear the truth. "Yeah, I mean it." His lips curled into a half smile.

"I think I could've learned a lot faster if you'd given me the chance."

"Jake wanted me to bring you along slowly," Russ admitted. "He wanted to be sure you knew what you were doing."

She stared at him, a look of distrust in her eyes.

"Why? Because he was hoping I'd change my mind?"

Russ didn't corroborate her statement. "You take it up with him." He gently patted the horse. "You had a lot to learn in the beginning, but you've come a long way."

Lynn swallowed hard as she watched Russ's big hand slide across the horse's hide. Her memory of how those same hands had slid along her skin made her spine tingle. "Casper has good 'horse sense.'" He'd been given the name Casper because he used to spook easily. He was a different horse now, and she was proud of his progress. "He's done most of the work." Shifting her stance, she ran her hand down the horse's mane.

"Don't sell yourself short. You have a natural talent that I've just helped develop."

She looked up at him then, and his gaze locked with hers. Dark and mysterious, it traveled over her body, making her insides turn to jelly. "Thanks," she replied, striving to keep her voice from revealing her thoughts.

Russ tamped down on his urge to touch her. Still, his gaze dropped to her mouth, and he remembered how sweet she'd tasted, wanted very badly to taste her again. Trying to keep his mind on business around her was a challenge. He wanted to sweep her off her feet and carry her to his bed, wanted to bury himself inside her so deep that his hunger would be assuaged.

Damn, he was losing his objectivity.

"He's ready to be returned to his owner," Russ commented.

"I know. I hate to see him go," she told him, her fondness for the horse showing in her eyes. She knew he'd be in good hands. His owner was a nearby rancher who'd recently lost his wife and was left trying to juggle ranching and raise three small children. He had the Bar M training his horses because he no longer had the time.

"I've contacted Dan Blake and arranged for him to come on Monday morning."

She broke eye contact with him. "I won't be here on Monday morning. Can you make it in the afternoon?" Turning away, she began unsaddling the horse.

Russ frowned. "What's so important that you can't be here?"

She shrugged, her back still to him. "I have plans in Crockett." Though she'd told him about her desire to start her own horse ranch, she didn't think he'd like the news that she'd stepped up her plans and was meeting the banker. She hadn't planned on going into it with Russ. It wasn't a concern of his, and she didn't need his interference.

He picked up on her evasive tone, and he wondered what she was hiding. "Change them," he ordered.

Lynn rounded and faced him squarely, putting her hands on her hips. "I *can't* change them." She could tell from his stance that he didn't like her answer. This was the Russ she knew, obstinate and thoroughly uncooperative. He made her want to scream.

"Then you won't be here."

"That's not fair," Lynn complained, her lips thinning. "I should be here. I'm the one who trained Casper. Can't you ask Mr. Blake to come in the afternoon?"

"Give me a good reason why I should." His tone was uncompromising. He wanted to know what she was up to, and he planned to force the issue until she told him.

Lynn struggled to hold on to her temper. "If you must know, I have an appointment with Linwood Finney at the bank to talk with him about a loan." She grabbed the saddle and pulled it from the horse, then struggled to get a better grasp on it.

Russ wrestled the saddle from her. "So that's what this is all about." He should have figured as much. He'd given her a couple of days to settle down, and instead of her coming around to his way of thinking, damn her, she'd gone ahead with her own plans for her future.

"Yes, I called him a few days ago and made an appointment to talk with him on Monday morning." She followed him as he started walking away from her.

"And have you spoken to your brothers yet?" He tossed the saddle down in the barn. A puff of dust and tiny bits of hay flew into the air.

"You know I haven't. Jake isn't due back until Saturday, and I want to talk to him and Ryder together. I decided I'd talk to Mr. Finney first, get the loan, then tell Jake and Ryder of my plans." Though her brothers loved her, they'd never agree to letting her live on her own. Not unless she could show them she was prepared and ready.

Russ grunted. She had it all figured out, and she'd cut him from her plans like he meant nothing to her. He should have felt relieved. So why wasn't he? Why was he annoyed as hell that he didn't matter to her?

"Do what you want, but I'm not changing the appointment," he snapped.

"Sometimes you are the most stubborn man!" Her

eyes were full of fire as she regarded him. How in her right mind had she ever let herself become involved with him?

"Well, hell, sweetheart, you sure aren't always a picnic!"

Lynn stared into his icy gaze. "Fine, I'll change the damn appointment." She stalked to the door and left without saying another word.

Later that evening, she watched from the office window as Russ came out of his room. He was still dressed in jeans, and he had on a gray T-shirt. He settled a Houston Astros baseball cap on his head as he walked toward his truck. Her heartbeat quickened as he climbed in and started it.

Where was he going? To see a woman?

Did he have a female companion in town, or possibly in San Luis? Well, so what if he did? It was really no concern of hers. They weren't a couple. They were…well, she wasn't sure what they were. She fingered the diamond on her hand, then raised it to her face to study it.

They were engaged.

Her chest ached. It wasn't the first time she'd seen him leave the ranch at night. Before she'd wondered where he went, but now she was downright curious. Was all that talk about getting married to protect her reputation lip service after all? Because of the situation they were in, he really had no business going out with other women. Not until this whole engagement mess was over and behind them.

Lynn watched his taillights disappear from view, and she reminded herself that she had her own agenda, and it didn't include Russ. It shouldn't really matter to her where he was going. She shouldn't care.

But she did.

It was then she knew she was getting in too deep where Russ was concerned. She needed to take a step back and distance herself emotionally from him.

Before it was too late and she lost her heart to him.

"Married?" Catherine McCall squealed, hugging her son, Matthew, to her. She and Jake had just returned from their honeymoon, and everyone was gathered around them on the front porch. "Really? You're serious?"

Russ had seen the newlyweds arrive in the Cessna six-seater, and figuring it wouldn't be long before the news of his engagement to Lynn reached them, he'd walked up to the house to join in greeting them. Ashley, bless her heart, hadn't even given Jake and Catherine time to get into the house before she had blurted out the news of Russ and Lynn's engagement.

Now they were all standing on the wide front porch. Russ's chest tightened when he stepped closer to Lynn, a feeling that was becoming all too familiar when he was around her.

He wasn't sure how Jake was going to take the news. If his first reaction was anything like Ryder's, Russ wasn't going to leave Lynn alone to defend her actions. Of course, now they had the benefit of Jake not finding them in bed together, a detail he would no doubt be told eventually.

Russ stood behind Lynn and possessively put his hands on her shoulders. She glanced back at him and gave him a slight smile, and her expression told him she was glad that he was there. He gently squeezed her shoulders as he felt the full force of her oldest brother's speculative gaze.

Apparently, Lynn had also. As she faced Jake's suspicious stare, she inched backward into Russ's embrace, aligning her back against his chest, tucking the curve of her rear against him. The warmth of her body, the smell of her, enveloped him.

"That so?" Jake asked, and his tone held a trace of disbelief. It was obvious his question was directed at Russ and not Lynn.

Unintimidated, Russ returned an unwavering stare. "Yes." He wrapped his arms around Lynn, locking his hands together in front of her, and he pulled her closer.

"I can't believe it." It was obvious to everyone that he was having a difficult time dealing with the unexpected news. "You're in love with Lynn?" His tone was incredulous.

Russ suppressed his annoyance. Lynn was sweet, smart and downright pretty. Despite the fact that he'd been trapped into this fiasco, he couldn't understand why everyone seemed to find it difficult to believe he could have fallen for her. Or maybe they were having a hard time reconciling the fact that she was in love with him. That made more sense.

"As a matter of fact, I am," he stated. He was determined to protect her. If it wasn't for him, they wouldn't be in this predicament. To drive his point home, he nuzzled Lynn's neck. She trembled in his arms.

Catherine chuckled. "I told you, didn't I?" she said to Jake, drawing his attention. She looked at Lynn, her eyes twinkling with delight. "I *knew* something was happening between you two, and I even mentioned it to Jake while we were gone. I'm so happy for you.''

Russ let Lynn go as Catherine hugged her. She made a point to kiss his cheek, as well, then he put his arm around Lynn's waist.

''Um, thank you.'' Lynn could barely get the words out. Her entire body felt smothered by Russ's presence. She'd been surprised when she'd seen him come across the yard, more so when he'd come up behind her and held her against him.

''I guess congratulations are in order,'' Jake said, looking at Lynn. He turned his eyes on Russ. ''I'd like to have a private word with you.''

''Oh, no you don't,'' Lynn stated, and she held on to Russ's arm when he started to move away from her. ''You don't have a thing to say about this, Jake.''

''Yes, I do.''

''I'm old enough to know what I want,'' she insisted.

''It's okay.'' Russ cupped the back of Lynn's neck, drawing her attention.

''But—''

''I'll handle it,'' he told her, stroking her skin with his thumb. She turned toward him, her expression worried. ''We'll be right back.'' He kissed her briefly on the lips, then stepped away from her and followed Jake down the steps toward the corral. Ryder went along with them. Matthew, who considered himself included, was clearly unhappy when he was asked to stay with the women.

Ashley grabbed Catherine's hand. ''There's a lot of planning to do. Lynn wants to get married within six months. I told her how excited we'd be to plan a wedding, since both you and I had a spur-of-the-moment affair.''

"Oh, yes!" Catherine smiled, excited about the prospect. "This will be so much fun." They took off together, and Lynn had no choice but to follow. She glanced back at Jake, Ryder and Russ, who were standing beside the corral talking, and she wondered exactly what her brothers were up to.

"Have you decided on where you're going to have the ceremony?" Catherine asked, then before Lynn could answer, she went on, "What about a dress? Have you looked for one, yet?"

Shaking her head, Lynn trailed behind them into the large den. "No, I—"

In her excitement, Catherine didn't give her the chance to answer. "Great! I want to go with you to shop for it. I know a really wonderful place. There's a new shop that's just opened in San Luis. If we don't find one there, we can go to San Antonio."

"Well, I—"

"Oh, and the cake! Are you going to use Mrs. Cherry or buy it somewhere else?"

"I haven't decided where—"

"I made some notes," Ashley said, interrupting her. "I know we've always used Mrs. Cherry because there's no bakery in Crockett, but there's that new place that opened near Ozona. I think we should see what they have."

Lynn started to speak again, but never had the chance. Ashley and Catherine were talking excitedly about *her* wedding plans, and she couldn't seem to get a word in between them. As they continued to chat, she wandered over to the window. Looking out, she saw Jake, Ryder and Russ still talking.

She was going to personally wring Jake's neck for embarrassing her. Though she loved her brothers, she wasn't happy knowing they still thought it necessary to protect her. She was a grown woman, after all. She was perfectly capable of making her own decisions—and that included marrying Russ!

"What do you think, Lynn?"

Lynn turned when she heard her name called, her expression blank. "What?"

Catherine walked over and glanced out the window. Spotting Russ and the other men, she laughed. "Oh, so that's where your mind was. Tell me, how did you ever break through that wall that surrounds him?"

Her cheeks burning, Lynn moved quickly away from the window and across the room.

Grinning, Ashley volunteered, "Oh, I bet even I can tell you that."

Shooting a silencing look at Ashley, Lynn cleared her throat. "Um, what were you trying to ask me?" she asked, steering the conversation away from where it was headed. The last thing she wanted to do was to stand there and hear Ashley tell Catherine how Ryder had walked in on her and Russ in bed together.

Catherine paused, trying to digest the direction of their conversation. She ended up answering Lynn. "Oh, we were thinking about an all-day shopping trip this weekend. We could start in San Luis, then drive into San Antonio." Her voice rose a pitch as her excitement built. "We can look at invitations to get an idea of what you'd like."

"And flowers," Ashley added. "Have you thought about the kind of flowers you want? There are so many kinds to choose from. I've got some wonderful ideas already jotted down on a pad in the office. Why don't I go get it?''

''Wait!'' Lynn said. Ashley stopped in her tracks, and Lynn stared at them both. Her life was getting more and more out of control. This pretend wedding was taking on a life of its own. ''Um, not now. I've, uh, got some things to do.'' She edged toward the door. ''We'll make definite plans later.''

Before either woman could speak, Lynn rushed out and escaped to the sanctity of her room, slamming the door behind her, then taking a huge breath. She *had* to get some kind of grip back on her life! Why did everyone else want to control *her* destiny? And why couldn't her brothers stay out of her personal business?

Well, she had news for them all. She was going to claim her life back.

Immediately!

She'd changed her appointment with Linwood Finney. She'd hoped to get one later in the week, but he'd already had plans to go out of town. A new appointment had been scheduled for her Tuesday morning. Getting a loan was going to be the first definite step in her plans. Once she got past that hurdle, they'd all see that she could take care of herself.

And that included Russ.

''Have a seat, Lynn, and I'll let Linwood know you're here.'' Sadie Andrews waved her hand at a set of brown leather chairs. Lynn nodded and clutching a large envelope, sat on the edge of her seat, anxious to get her meeting started. Once she had approval of a loan, her plans would start taking definite shape and some degree of normalcy would return in her life.

She'd be able to go home, pretend to break up with Russ, then move forward with her plans.

She looked up as Linwood Finney walked into the room. He was a tall, thin man in his early fifties. A friend of her parents, Lynn had known him since she was a little girl. Though she could've shown up in jeans, she'd taken the time to put on a dress and sandals. Absently, she ran her fingers through her hair, then stood and took his hand when he offered it.

"Mr. Finney."

"Lynn, sweetheart, it's good to see you." The banker held her hand in his a moment, and his eyes were as warm and friendly as his greeting. "Come on into my office where we can talk."

She followed him into an adjoining room and took a seat in front of his small wooden desk. Papers were piled high on one side, and a framed picture of his family stood prominently on the other. He took a seat and smiled, then leaned forward on his elbows, giving her his complete attention.

"Now, what can I do for you?"

Lynn jumped right into her reason for the appointment, then proceeded to expand on her plans. As she talked, she opened the envelope and pulled out a manila folder, continuing to outline her ideas as she talked. She'd given her plans a lot of thought, had taken the time to formulate a proposal. She smiled and handed him a copy.

Mr. Finney slipped a pair of reading glasses on the bridge of his nose and was silent as he studied the paper. "Well, it appears you've put a lot of work into this idea." He went on to ask a few questions, and Lynn filled in further details. When she finished talking, he laid the paper on his desktop. "I'm impressed," he told her. "How long have you been working on this?"

"I've always loved horses. I started thinking about training them during my last year of school, then one thing led to another, and I figured it'd be great to have my own ranch." She smiled again. He seemed genuinely impressed with her detailed proposal. Adrenaline caused blood to rush through her veins.

Mr. Finney nodded. "Well, I think we'll be able to work something out without too much difficulty."

"Great!" Lynn answered, obviously pleased. "Thank you." She closed the folder and looked down on the floor for her purse.

"I'll have Sadie get the paperwork together. It should be ready in a few days. I'll give you a call, and we'll set a date for you and Jake to come back in and sign the forms."

Lynn stopped in the process of getting up. She redirected her attention to the banker. "What?"

He sat back in his chair. "It won't take too long to draw—"

"I'm sorry," she interrupted. "Why do you need Jake here?"

"You'll need Jake to come in and cosign the loan."

She sat up straighter. "Why? I mean, I own part of the ranch, don't I?"

"Of course you have an interest in the ranch, Lynn, but Jake controls the assets, as well as making all decisions on the finances. He has since your parents passed away. I can't give you this loan without his signature."

She barely managed to cover her astonishment and struggled to keep her composure. "I see."

"Should I go ahead and have the papers drawn up?"

Lynn swallowed past her disappointment. There was no way Jake was going to go for this idea. "Why don't you wait for a few days? I'll get back to you on it." She wasn't about to admit that she hadn't talked her plans over with her brother.

"Okay, fine. I'll put this in a pending file, and you give me a call when you're ready to move forward."

Lynn nodded, then quickly got to her feet. Suddenly she felt as if she was suffocating. She had to get out of there. "Yes. Thank you for seeing me." With her purse and the envelope in her hands, she went to the door before he was out of his seat.

Mr. Finney stood. "It was my pleasure."

Barely paying attention, Lynn waved goodbye and rushed out the door. She didn't look at Sadie as she left, but kept her eyes focused on the door. Her insides ached with discouragement as she climbed behind the wheel of her pickup. After she closed the door, she started the engine, then pulled away from the curb in front of the bank.

Tears of frustration welled in her eyes. She hadn't planned on this obstacle at all. Damn it all, she felt totally stupid. Sniffing, she tried hard to keep her emotions under control, but it was so hard. This was more than a mere setback. She knew Jake. He was never going to agree to cosign a loan. Despite the fact that she'd formed an impressive proposal, having her own ranch was not what he wanted.

And because of this stupid pretend engagement, she couldn't even discuss it with him! And when she broke it off, she'd look even more like she didn't know what she wanted.

As she drove home, Lynn wished more than anything that she had somewhere else to go. She didn't
feel like facing anyone. A lump lodged in her throat
as she passed the corrals and pulled into the yard,
stopping the truck in front of the house. For a moment
she just sat there slumped in the seat, staring at nothing.

It wasn't fair, she cried out silently. Her decisions,
her course in life, should be for her to decide. Not
the bank's, and certainly not Jake's. Drawing in a
deep breath, she glanced out the windshield, and she
was relieved to see no one in sight. She had to get
out, but she just couldn't summon up the courage to
go into the house. The last thing she wanted was to
run into Ashley or Catherine, or heaven forbid, one
of her brothers. More than anything, she wanted to be
alone.

Summoning the will to be strong, she decided to
saddle a horse and take a ride and think about her
options. Not that she had any. Where was she going
to go from here? Jake was used to telling her what
she could or couldn't do. When he eventually learned
that she wasn't going to marry Russ, he'd start all
over again about her furthering her education.

Her chest tightened, and pain seared her heart.
Tears threatened again as she climbed from the truck
and crossed the yard, heading for the barn. She
clamped her lips together, and her jaw ached from the
pressure of holding her emotions in.

Opening the barn door, she started to go inside, but
was startled when she smacked into someone.

Oh, dammit, not Russ!

She didn't have to look up to know he was exactly
who she'd run into. She especially didn't want to see

him—another reminder of someone wanting to tell her what she could or couldn't do.

Barely holding herself together, she glanced up at him, then just as quickly turned her gaze away. "I'm sorry," she whispered, then damned the way her voice cracked.

Grabbing her arm, Russ steadied her, realizing immediately that she was trembling. Frowning with concern, he studied her delicate features. "Lynn, what's wrong?"

She shook her head. "Nothing, I—" Her throat felt clogged, and she couldn't get intelligible words to come out of her mouth. When she tried to move around him, he held on to her. She raised her arm and tried to shake free of his grasp. "Let me go."

Russ's jaw tightened. "Talk to me," he demanded. "What happened to upset you?"

She didn't say anything. She couldn't. If she tried to talk, she'd fall apart right in front of him. Pushing at his chest, she struggled to free herself. Russ subdued her by grasping both of her arms, preventing her escape.

"Did someone hurt you?" he demanded.

She stilled. Without looking at him, she slowly shook her head.

"Honey, are you hurt?"

Despite her attempt to stay in control, Lynn felt her composure shatter. With absolute dread, she raised her face to his. Before she could stop herself, she threw herself into his arms and burst into tears.

Eight

Russ felt every muscle in his body tighten as Lynn pressed herself against him. She was shaking uncontrollably, and her crying intensified as he tried to calm her. He'd remembered that she'd had that appointment in town. Something must have happened there, he figured.

But what?

He looked her over closely. She was wearing a blue, short-sleeved embroidered-yoke dress. He didn't see any bruises on her skin. She didn't look hurt, just terribly upset. Regardless of what had transpired, at that moment, he knew one thing for damn sure. He'd personally find the person responsible for hurting her and beat him within an inch of his life.

Slowly massaging her back, he let her cry, and she burrowed deeper against him, burying her face in his chest. Her shoulders shook, and she gasped for air. After fishing in his pocket and giving her a handkerchief, Russ held her closer, and despite her obvious pain, something inside him tightened, a feeling that ran deep enough to scare him.

He was beginning to care for her. Lately, instead of avoiding her, he'd caught himself searching her out. When he should have been keeping his hands to himself, he'd used every opportunity to touch her.

"Shh..." Holding her against him, he brushed her short blond hair with his chin, and he murmured softly to her, "Honey, talk to me. Tell me what happened, and I'll try to help you."

Lynn sobbed even harder.

"Come on," he said, his voice coaxing as he led her away from the barn and the house. "I can't help you if you won't talk to me."

She let him draw her away without argument, and her docile manner was further proof that something had happened to disturb her deeply. Normally when it came to him, Lynn never did anything without putting up a fuss.

He'd learned quickly enough that she didn't like being told what to do. That had been the source of their heated discussions in the past, and would probably be the source of more in the future, he thought sardonically. They slowly made their way around one of the corrals and continued walking until Russ stopped near a grove of trees a distance away from the barn. Once there, he lowered them both to the ground, then settled himself against the base of a tree to support his back.

When he pulled her to sit beside him, she leaned her shoulder against his chest and allowed him to put his arm around her. Her breathing started to slow, and she sucked in a deep breath. After agonizing moments of silence, she finally spoke.

"I'm sorry," she whispered, and her voice was eerily quiet. "I didn't mean to fall apart on you like that."

Russ continued to move his hand in a circular pattern on her back. "It's all right, honey. Want to talk about it?"

She sniffed, then swiped at her eyes with her hand. "No." Then a soft-spoken, "Maybe."

"Do you want me to go and break someone's legs?" he asked, and the lift in his voice undermined the seriousness of his words.

She gave a halfhearted chuckle that came from deep inside her throat. "No, but thank you for offering."

Russ remained silent, knowing she'd talk if she wanted. He could hear the distant sounds of cattle, and could see Ryder and Jake pull into the yard, but he knew that he and Lynn were pretty much hidden from their view by the fences and the animals.

His fingers caressed the back of her neck, and she looked up at him, her gaze drawn to his mouth. At that moment his gaze snared hers, and embarrassed, she quickly averted her eyes.

Lynn eased away, sitting across from him. She straightened her dress, arranging it over her legs, then slipped off her sandals. The heat of his gaze made her skin prickle. Though love was not a factor in their relationship, she felt a strong desire to be held and comforted by him. Picking at the grass, she chanced a glance at him. He was regarding her silently, his eyes questioning.

"I'm not going to get the bank loan," she confessed, and again the pain of seeing her dreams disappear caused her heart to ache. She told him the details of her conversation with Linwood Finney, the words pouring out of her. "I feel so stupid. I didn't realize that Jake would have to sign for me."

"Ah." Russ felt bad for her. Even worse, he'd figured she'd run into this kind of obstacle, but deciding she wouldn't listen to him, he hadn't even tried to warn her.

The tone of his voice made her look at him. "You knew that was a possibility, didn't you?" Though her voice remained soft, there was an underlying accusation in her tone.

"I wondered," was all he said. He supposed that in the back of his mind, he'd hoped that once starting her own ranch was no longer a factor, she'd start accepting the fact that they were going to get married.

"But you didn't say anything to me?"

"You had your mind made up. Most of the time we're at cross-purposes, so I doubt you would have believed me."

He was right, of course, and she couldn't deny it. "I don't know what I'm going to do now. I'll have to think of another way, I guess." She sniffed again, then wiped at her eyes with her hands. "Do you know what it's like to want something so bad that you can taste it?"

"Yeah."

He didn't elaborate, and she lifted her face and looked directly at him, her eyes wide with curiosity. "Really?"

Russ's lips twisted as he toyed with the idea of revealing his own plans for the future. They wouldn't sound like much, but they were important to him. "I have a piece of land. It's not far from here actually. I figure by next year, I'll have enough money to stock it."

"With horses? You're going to start your own ranch?" She stared at him, mystified. She'd had no idea at all that Russ would ever leave the Bar M. The thought of him doing so caused a new and different kind of ache in her chest.

"Eventually," he admitted with what seemed like reluctance.

She studied him intently, wanting to know more. "Is that what you did before you moved here?"

"I worked on ranches, yes." He looked away and stared off toward the sky. Why had he let her lead him into this conversation? he wondered. He usually wasn't comfortable sharing his thoughts. Finding it easy to talk to Lynn, considering their earlier altercations, both surprised and worried him.

"In Montana?"

"Mostly."

"Is that where you grew up?"

"Yeah."

"Do your parents still live there?" she asked without bothering to mask her inquisitiveness.

Russ leaned forward and rested his arm on his knee. "I lived with an aunt for most of my life. My mother dumped me there when I was a kid and took off on her own. I never saw her again." He didn't look at her then, couldn't stand the thought of Lynn feeling sorry for him. He wasn't the first kid who'd been abandoned, and sadly, he wouldn't be the last.

Lynn didn't look away from him. Instead, she kept her gaze steady, and she guessed that possibly the way he was raised was the reason he remained a man unto himself. "What was your aunt like?"

He shook his head, and his attempt at a smile fizzled. "She was a hard woman. I don't think she meant to be unkind, but she wasn't exactly thrilled to have me. She'd lived by herself for many years in a small town. People there would've disapproved of her if she hadn't kept me."

Which meant that she'd kept him because she'd *had* to, Lynn surmised. That or his aunt would have had to face the ridicule of her friends and neighbors. Forgetting her own problems, Lynn's heart throbbed for the little boy he'd once been and how terribly sad it must have been for him to lose his mother and be forced to live with an unfeeling woman who hadn't wanted him.

"So what happened when you grew up?"

"I left the day I finished high school. I worked where I could get a job, and I scnt money to my aunt to pay her back for the inconvenience of raising me." He swore softly, then looked back at Lynn. "Eventually I got married."

Lynn studied the wounded expression in his eyes, and it told her so much more than his words. She'd had no idea, of course, that he'd been married before. The thought of him loving another woman, marrying another woman, bothered her in ways she wasn't ready to explore.

"What happened?"

"She found someone to keep her company when I wasn't around." His tone held a bitter twist. "I probably wouldn't have ever found out, except she got pregnant and I found out it wasn't mine."

She touched his arm. He stiffened for a moment,

then appeared to relax slightly. "I'm sorry. That must've been horrible," she told him.

"I got over it." His tone was indifferent. He'd gotten over Candace's betrayal, and he'd moved on. He hadn't expected, hadn't *wanted* any more from life than to live it peacefully.

By himself.

Until he'd made love to Lynn.

She made him want things he could never have.

"Did you?" It seemed to her that though he probably wouldn't admit it, he had it all bottled up inside him. His solitary existence was proof that he didn't trust anyone but himself.

"Yeah, I did," he told her, and his tone held a warning to let it drop. "I moved on, settled here, and if all goes right, I'll have my own ranch one day."

Lynn considered pushing him into talking more because there was so much more she wanted to know about him, but his scowl stopped her. She slid her palm across his arm and rested her hand on his. "Can I see it?"

"What?" Russ asked suspiciously, his skin heating from her touch. But instead of withdrawing from her like he should have, instead of keeping his hands off her, he linked his fingers with hers. Her skin felt soft and delicate, and his gut knotted.

"Your ranch. Will you take me to see it?"

"Why?"

She tilted her head, and a smile appeared on her lips. "Because I'd like to see it."

Russ looked around him at the expansive operation of the Bar M. "It's nothing like this place." He wasn't ashamed of it, but he didn't want her to get the wrong idea. The house needed work to make it livable. He spent most of his spare time there working on it, and there was still a lot to do.

"That doesn't matter," she assured him. "I'd still like to see it."

He didn't understand why she'd be interested, but he shrugged and said, "If you're sure you want to."

"How about this weekend?" she pressed, not giving him a chance to change his mind. He nodded, and she grinned. "Great!" She got to her feet, then realized he was still holding her hand. Blushing, she disentangled her fingers from his and picked up her sandals. "I guess we'd better get back."

"Yeah." Russ nodded and stood. He gave her a half grin. "Wouldn't want your family to think I was taking advantage of you out here in the grass," he teased.

She picked up on the fact that he was baiting her. "Or that I was taking advantage of you," she replied tartly, then she walked away and left him standing there.

"We have *got* to do something about this engagement!" Lynn slammed the door to Russ's truck so hard it rattled the window glass. "Ashley and Catherine are like vicious pit bulls." Since he'd promised to take her, she'd been looking forward to seeing his ranch, but her latest conversation with her sisters-in-law about her supposed wedding plans had stolen some of her enthusiasm. She couldn't get away from the house fast enough.

Russ shot her a curious look as he pushed down the gas pedal. "What happened?"

She glared at him as he slowly pulled away from the house. "What do you think? The two barracudas that I'm living with are out for my blood." He chuckled, and she shot him a hot glance as they traveled farther away from the ranch. "Go ahead. Laugh. You won't think it's funny when they start on you." She slumped down in the seat, then crossed her arms over her chest.

"They keep asking me if we've set a date for the wedding. You'd think they'd have more important things to think about. But nooooo. It's, have you and Russ talked any more about setting a date? When are you going to decide? We need to know something definite. Do you think you can tell us something specific in the next few days? And on and on and on. It's driving me crazy!" Her tirade ended as she ran out of breath.

"Actually, I know how you feel. Your brother cornered me yesterday," Russ admitted.

Her head whipped in his direction. "Jake?"

"Yeah. You shouldn't be so surprised. I told you how your brothers would react when they found out we were sleeping together."

"But we're not," she protested, then a flush rose to her cheeks. "I mean, we're not now."

Russ's lip twisted at the reminder. It had been days since he'd touched her. Long, difficult days of spending time with her and wanting so bad to kiss her that he ached with it. "They don't know that. They want me to make an honest woman of you. We're gonna have to set a date and stick by it."

"No!"

Gritting his teeth, Russ tried to hold on to his temper. "You can fight this all you want, but it's gonna happen."

"There's got to be another solution. We just have to think of something."

"Yeah? Like what?" he demanded.

She shrugged her shoulders. "I don't know, but I'll come up with something."

"Try coming up with a short date. That'll satisfy everyone."

"Not me!" She lifted her chin defiantly. Marrying Russ, even for a little while, would undermine her desire to control her life. That wasn't an option.

His expression stony, Russ shifted his attention back to the road and turned onto a narrow dirt drive. The truck bounced over a few ruts in the path before he pulled to a stop in front of a large, two-story structure.

"You bought the Petersons' place?" she asked, looking around her, her eyes widening. He nodded and got out of the truck. She quickly followed. "Really?" Lynn was stunned. Though ten minutes away by car, the Peterson property line backed up to the McCalls', making it accessible by horseback.

He nodded and looked toward the two-story farmhouse. "It needs a lot of work, I know."

The old farmhouse stood before them. It was sturdily built with fluted columns and a slate roof. Two large dormers jutted out from the second floor. "It has so much character," she said with admiration.

"I ran into Peterson in town one day and he mentioned that he and his wife were moving back east to be with her mother who was ill. I told him I'd keep an eye on the place for him if he wanted. He said he was more interested in selling it, that he was getting too old to keep up with it and he didn't think they'd be coming back." He looked at the house and saw it through her eyes. Lynn was used to the best, and he figured the place looked pretty shabby to her.

"They had several kids. Didn't any of them want it?"

Russ walked up to the front door, which was in dire need of a coat of paint. He absently picked off a peeling gray chip. "His son got a job in the computer industry and lives somewhere in California, and both his daughters married and moved away."

"Oh." Lynn stepped onto the porch, then she waited for Russ to open the door.

"I decided to start doing repairs inside, but I hope to have it painted before winter sets in," he explained as they stepped inside. "I've been working on it now and then when I have some free time."

Looking around as she walked in, Lynn realized this was where Russ went on his time off. Had he come here the other night when she'd seen him leave the Bar M? The smell of fresh paint filled her nostrils as she walked through the rooms downstairs. She liked that he'd chosen a soft off-white color for the walls.

"Did they leave this furniture?" she asked, noticing that although the rooms weren't completely furnished, there were a few pieces of furniture in each room.

"They said they didn't have room to take it all and left some behind."

"Did you put this in?" she asked, admiring the bannister as they walked up the wooden staircase. A couple of the steps creaked under her feet.

He ran his hand across the smooth, dark-stained wood. "I've got some equipment out in the barn," he admitted a little reluctantly.

"You *built* this?" Fascinated, she inspected his work. "It's beautiful!" she exclaimed. Automatically her gaze went to his hands, the same hands that had intimately caressed her body. Of course, she'd known he was talented in *that* department, but she'd had no idea that he could create such exquisite woodwork. Realizing where her thoughts had turned, she gulped. "Is this where you go at night?"

Russ's expression turned thoughtful. "Where I go?" he repeated.

Too late, Lynn realized what she'd asked. "I saw you leaving the Bar M the other night," she admitted.

"And you wondered where I was going?"

Annoyed by the satisfied grin on his face, Lynn rolled her eyes. "Not exactly."

"Yes, you did," Russ said.

"Okay, so what if I did? You were the one so determined to make people believe that this engagement is real. I thought—"

"That I was going to see a woman?" he supplied, and appeared quite pleased that she'd been thinking about him and where he'd been going. "Well, I wasn't. I'm not involved with anyone, so you don't have to worry about it."

Lynn frowned at him. "I wasn't worried." She stepped over a freshly painted piece of baseboard.

"Uh-huh." He took her hand and pulled her along behind him, leading her though the rest of the upstairs, showing her the bedrooms.

Each room was in a different stage of repair, except for the master bedroom, which seemed to be finished. "You've done a lot of work," she said.

"A little here and there. I've been concentrating on the kitchen, trying to get it up-to-date. C'mon, I'll show you." He indicated for her to follow him down yet another staircase at the back of the house which led into the large kitchen. There was lots of cabinet space, and the range had been replaced. The sink was white enamel, and the cabinet beneath was open, the pipes taken apart.

"You're doing the plumbing?"

"I've had quite a few odd jobs. I picked up a little of this and that along the way."

Lynn nodded. Before he'd come to the Bar M, it seemed he'd been pretty much a drifter. She turned around in a circle. The room still needed a lot of work, but it was coming along nicely considering only one person was working on it. There was a sturdy wooden kitchen table in the corner, and most of the curtains had been left.

Suddenly, an idea took shape in her mind, and she spun back around to face him. "Oh my gosh, Russ, this is the answer to our problem!"

She had that look on her face that warned him he wasn't going to like what she was going to say. "I don't see how."

Her mind began to churn even faster. "We can pretend to elope, live here a while until things cool down. After a while, we'll pretend to get a divorce, and by then I'll have figured out a way to start my own place."

"We can't do that!"

"I know it sounds kind of crazy, but it'll work."

"It won't work, and I'm not going to go along with it so just forget it." He admired her tenacity when it came to starting her own horse ranch, but all he could think about was that her future plans didn't involve him. He started out of the room, and she grabbed for his arm, but missed. She had to practically run to catch up with him.

"Wait! Listen!"

Russ abruptly stopped in his tracks and turned to confront her. Lynn's momentum carried her smack into his arms. He tensed, then swiftly set her away from him. "No. End of story." His hands went to his hips.

"Russ, just think about it!" she pleaded.

"I'm not going to play these games with you anymore, and I'm not lying to your family, either." He was already in way over his head. If he went along with her latest scheme, Russ could just imagine that he'd be the laughingstock of Crockett when the truth came out.

And eventually it would, no matter how hard they tried to keep it quiet. He'd already lived through one bad experience. His wife's infidelity was the reason he'd left his hometown. Now, ready to settle down and live his life in peace, he'd invested everything he'd earned into this land and this house. He wasn't going to risk losing it by going along with her crazy plan.

"But, it'll get Ashley and Catherine off my back, and Jake and Ryder will leave you alone. They'll think we're already married and quit expecting us to set a date. It's the perfect answer!"

"It's not even close to being the perfect answer. As a matter of fact, it's damned near the dumbest thing I've heard come out of your mouth! It's right up there with, *'we're engaged,'* which started this whole fiasco." There was no way he was going along with it.

"All right," she conceded. "Then you think of

something because I can't take the pressure much longer!'' she challenged, irritated that he wouldn't even consider the idea.

Russ looked directly into her eyes. As he saw it, there was only one way out of the whole mess.

''Okay, let's really elope.''

''What?'' Realizing he was dead serious, Lynn stared at him wide-eyed and stunned.

''You heard me. Let's elope. We can drive to San Luis and get married right there at the courthouse. We'll tell your family the truth for a change, that we got married. The end result will be the same—they'll leave us alone.''

''You want us to *really* get married?''

He nodded, not really understanding her surprise. He'd been telling her that he was going to marry her for days. Though she'd fought him all along, Russ still had every intention of following through on his word. Maybe now she would take him seriously. If he could get her to agree, he'd have lived up to his promise to her brother.

''And live together? Here?'' she squeaked.

''It makes more sense than that cockamamy scheme of yours.''

Lynn backed up a step. ''I don't know.''

''It'll also solve our problem if you're pregnant.''

''I'm not pregnant!'' she insisted. She'd assured him that being anxious could cause her period to be late. She didn't want him to know that she was beginning to worry about it herself.

''So you keep saying. At least this way, we'll be married if you are,'' he reasoned.

''I guess it could work.''

''It's the right thing to do. You can't like keeping

the truth from your family. I have this house so we can live here for a while, then when things cool down and we know pregnancy is no longer a factor, we'll call it off.''

Lynn hesitated a moment longer, then said, ''Okay, I'll agree on one condition.''

''Name it,'' Russ said, ready to agree to anything if she'd just go along with him for a change.

''We don't sleep together.''

''We don't?''

''No. Neither of us wants things more complicated than they already are. You don't really want to be married, and neither do I. If we don't sleep together after we're married, we could get an annulment rather than a divorce.''

Of course, she'd have to control her attraction to him, keep him at a distance. She'd already put her heart at risk by making love with him again. Any further intimacy between them could lead to her falling in love with him, and that was something she wanted no part of. She wasn't going to fall in love with Russ. She wasn't going to jeopardize her dream of running her own life and starting her own horse ranch. But marrying Russ *would* buy her time to make some new plans, she reasoned as she waited for his answer.

Russ regarded her with uncertainty. Though ready to agree to anything she asked, she'd caught him off guard with that one. He had to admit that it made sense. He'd do well to remember that he needed to keep his distance from her.

He didn't like the idea of keeping their plan of getting an annulment from her family, but it couldn't be helped. He'd wanted to protect her reputation, as well as his own, and now she was willing to meet him halfway. ''All right,'' he agreed, knowing her condition was going to be hard to abide by, but determined to keep his word.

Well, hell, at least he'd have done right by her. It was a means to an end.

In theory, it would work.

So why did he feel like his heart was being ripped out of his chest?

Nine

Lynn stared out of the blurry side window of the truck as Russ pulled to a stop in front of the courthouse in San Luis. Rain pelted the windows, and she shivered when a violent bolt of lightning streaked across the sky.

Not exactly how she'd pictured her wedding day.

Of course, it wasn't like this was a *real* wedding. She and Russ weren't going to be sharing the same bed, after all. Stealing a glance at him, a part of her regretted making that stipulation. They'd get married, and for the next few months, they were more or less going to live as man and wife—at least in the literal sense. Her desire for his touch was something she'd have to work on. She'd simply use mind over matter.

As if that's going to work.

Okay, so maybe she'd gotten herself into yet another predicament, but she'd handle it somehow. A loud crack of thunder boomed and Lynn jumped. The weather had provided them with the perfect opportunity to slip away from the ranch for the morning. However, if it cleared up, they'd have to try and catch up on things this afternoon, so they were under pressure to get this done and return home.

Since they'd decided to elope, they'd been sneaking away from the Bar M, using every free minute possible to make Russ's farmhouse livable. She and Russ had actually managed to get along with each other through the fixing-up process. The Petersons had done what was necessary to keep it up, but the rooms hadn't been painted in years. Russ had been determined to get as much done as possible before they moved in.

Lynn had thought it was a good idea until she found herself imagining what it would be like to live there permanently with Russ. Her heart was constantly in turmoil, confused by her desire to be with him, and her need for independence and control. She couldn't sacrifice what she'd been fighting for, not even for a chance at winning Russ's heart.

And a slim chance was all it would be. He was only marrying her out of honor, out of a sense of doing what he felt was right. He'd told her more than once he was protecting his own reputation as well as hers.

He didn't love her. She wasn't foolish enough to think that he ever could. He'd said little on the ride to the courthouse, and that had been fine with her. The whole thing seemed a bit surreal.

"Wait here. I'll come around and get the door," he told her as he reached for the handle.

Lynn nodded. He grabbed an umbrella from the

floorboard and got out, popping it open as he trotted around the truck. She opened her door as he came closer, then hurried out beside him. Russ tucked her next to him, and together they ran through the downpour to the entrance of the courthouse.

Their clothes were practically soaked from the knees down as they rushed toward the gray stone building. Lynn shivered as they stepped inside. Her heart hammered as Russ talked to a receptionist, then led her down a wide hallway to a wooden door. Opening it, he stepped aside for Lynn to enter, and together they approached the first desk they reached. A white-haired woman with glasses perched on the end of her nose looked up at them, her expression expectant.

"May I help you?" she asked, and her smile was welcoming.

Lynn felt her throat close, and she looked to Russ.

"Yes. We're, uh, here to get a marriage license." He reached for her hand and held it in his, wishing the whole experience was over.

Lynn nervously fingered the folds of her simple white dress as he took the papers to fill out. She'd felt a little silly when she'd chosen it from her closet, but Russ's quick notice of it when he'd arrived to pick her up eased her anxiousness a little. She was equally glad that he'd donned black dress pants and a soft blue dress shirt.

"Oh, yes, I can tell. You have that look about you."

Both Lynn and Russ looked at each other. She giggled at the way his brows came together.

"Well, now, you've come to the right place. There are a few forms to fill out." The woman reached over and took some papers out of a folder. "Here they are.

Each of you will need to fill out information on this form, then we'll need both of your signatures on this one.'' She passed the papers and two pens to Russ, then indicated the empty table and chairs in the corner of the room. ''You can fill them out right there if you like.''

Russ nodded, then steered Lynn toward the table where they both took a seat. He handed her a pen and one of the papers, then began filling out his information. When finished, he passed it to her to do the same. Lynn quickly filled out her information, then they signed where indicated and returned to the desk.

''All right. I'll have your license ready in just a few minutes. You'll be on your way in no time. You do realize there's a three-day waiting period?''

Lynn glanced at Russ and saw he was as surprised as she was. ''There is? You mean we can't get married right now?''

''In a hurry, huh?'' She chuckled. ''Well, you can go before the judge and ask him to waive the waiting period,'' she informed them.

''All right,'' Russ replied, wondering why he hadn't at least called to check out the process. ''Where do we do that?'' he asked as the woman gave him the license.

She gave him the directions to the judge's courtroom. ''You may have to wait a few minutes if he's busy.''

Russ folded the paper and took Lynn's hand again. ''Is he the one who'll marry us?''

''Oh, no, honey, he only does the waivers.''

Russ frowned again. How could getting married be so difficult? ''Who do we see to get married today?''

''Well, I wish you'd have called before coming

here. District Judge Kinney can marry you, but he's in court right now. You're welcome to wait, of course.''

"Do you know how long it'll be?"

The woman shook her head. "I'm sorry, no. It could be fifteen minutes, or it could just as well be hours. There's no way to tell about these things."

Lynn turned toward Russ. "What now?"

"Let's go upstairs and see about the waiver," he suggested. "Thank you," he called to the woman as they left.

After waiting over two hours, they finally saw the judge and received a waiver of the waiting period. That left deciding on who would perform the ceremony.

''We could wait. She said the other judge has been in court all morning and it's already been another two hours. Maybe it won't be much longer,'' Lynn commented as they left the courtroom.

Russ glanced at his watch. "We've already been gone most of the morning from the ranch, and we really have to get back.'' He forced a smile. He hated the idea of putting off the ceremony until they could get away again. He didn't want to take a chance on Lynn changing her mind. Unfortunately, it didn't look like they had much of a choice.

"We could check the yellow pages. There's sure to be a justice of the peace listed.''

"By the time we find one, we'll have wasted more time," Russ told her, steering her toward the door. He popped open the umbrella again as they stepped outside the building and headed for the truck. "We'll just have to get away again somehow."

Once they were inside the truck and settled, he

started the engine and drove away from San Luis, heading toward the ranch. The windshield wipers worked furiously trying to keep up with the rain pounding the truck.

Shortly after they left town, Russ spotted a small church up ahead. "Look." He pointed toward it. "That might be the answer. There's a house next to that church. Maybe there's a preacher living there."

Lynn gulped air. "A preacher?" she repeated. "You're not serious!"

But she discovered he was very serious when he pulled the truck into the gravel driveway of the church. "Wait here," he commanded, then jumped out of the truck and left her before she had a chance to speak.

Sitting forward, her heart pounding, Lynn watched him run up on the porch and bang on the door of the house. Her stomach knotted when it opened and Russ began talking to a short, stout man. She saw Russ reach for his wallet, and her breath quickened as he handed the man some bills. Before she had a chance to find her breath, he was back at the truck.

"C'mon," he said, opening her door. He reached across Lynn for the umbrella. "We're getting married." He opened the umbrella and held it for her.

Lynn scrambled from the truck. "Here?"

"Why not?" Russ grabbed her hand and pulled her along.

"Because...because it's a church." She had to raise her voice to be heard over the thunder.

"So?" he whispered as he pulled her inside and closed the door.

He didn't understand.

Lynn clamped her lips together as she looked

around her. Stained glass windows with biblical scenes lined the outside walls. Rows of pews made from pine faced the front of the church where there was a small platform with chairs for the choir.

She stared at the altar, and a tingle ran down her spine.

She'd prepared herself for marrying Russ. She'd gone along with the idea because they'd decided on getting married by a judge or a justice of the peace.

Not by a preacher.

She stared at the preacher as she and Russ walked down the aisle to the front of the church. The man was standing beside a woman Lynn assumed was his wife. The woman was just about as stout as her husband, and she was smiling warmly. The two looked like they belonged together.

After welcoming them, the preacher introduced them both, then instructed Russ and Lynn to stand before the altar.

This can't really be happening!

Lynn's heart slammed against her ribs as Russ held her hand tight in his and looked into her eyes.

The preacher held their license in his hand as he began speaking. He must have married a lot of couples because he knew the words of the marriage ceremony by heart. Lynn felt panic rise inside her as he talked about love and commitment. As he neared the end of the ceremony, her entire body stiffened.

"Do you, Russ Logan, take this woman—"

Their gazes locked, and Lynn couldn't breathe. The tenderness in Russ's voice, the solemnness of tone as he promised to love and cherish her brought a lump to her throat.

When it came her turn to speak, she swallowed

hard and willed herself to repeat her marriage vows. Her body trembled when the preacher asked God to bless their union. How could He, when she and Russ would part in the near future, when their union was out of necessity and not born out of love?

"Do you have a ring?" the preacher asked.

Russ held out his hand, and Lynn's gaze fell on the two gold bands in his open palm. She hadn't even thought about the wedding band that matched her engagement ring, believing it wouldn't be used. And when had he bought a ring for himself? Before she had time to think about it further, Russ was claiming her hand and repeating after the preacher, then sliding the shining gold band on her finger.

Her hand shook uncontrollably as she took Russ's ring from the preacher and placed it on Russ's finger. Butterflies attacked her stomach. Her voice faltered as she tried to speak, then she managed to say the words expected of her.

Lynn heard the preacher pronounce them man and wife, and she knew what came next. She looked from the preacher to Russ. His eyes darkened as he drew her into his embrace. Suddenly, she was pressed against him, her body flush with his as he slipped his arms around her and dipped his head.

His mouth touched hers briefly, tenderly, and Lynn lost the ability to think. Her eyelids drifted shut, and the pleasure of his kiss reached out and stole a piece of her heart.

Panicking, she pulled away, careful not to look at Russ when she opened her eyes. She touched her mouth, still damp from his, and the taste of him lingered in her mind, crushing her determination to keep him at a distance.

As quickly and politely as possible, they thanked the preacher and his wife, then left the church. The rain had slacked a bit, but they were both quite wet from running back and forth in it. Russ opened her door for her, then got in behind the wheel.

"Okay, that's done," Lynn stated, making an effort to keep her tone even. She gave him a smile that didn't quite reach her eyes. For some silly reason, she felt like crying. But she wasn't going to.

Not here. Not now.

"Are you okay?" he asked, looking at her closely.

"Of course."

Russ's lips twisted as he studied her. Her hands were clenched, her back was stiff and she was practically glued to the door. She was everything but all right, he thought. He ran his hand along her hairline, brushing her bangs away from her face. She turned toward him, and he couldn't miss the shiny look in her eyes.

Touching her was a mistake.

Kissing her a few minutes ago had been an even bigger one. As he'd gazed into her eyes when she'd repeated her vows, he'd found himself wondering what it would be like if they were getting married for real. It was a foolish thought, he knew, wasted on something that could never be.

He didn't want to be married. He had nothing to offer a woman, nothing of himself to give.

And Lynn didn't want to be married, either. She wanted her freedom. She wanted to live her own life.

Gritting his teeth at the irony of their situation, he turned away, started the engine and headed for the Bar M. "I'm sorry about kissing you, if that's what you're upset about."

"I'm not upset."

"I know we made an agreement," he continued, feeling the need to justify his actions despite her quick denial. "I mean to abide by it. I just thought it would seem suspicious if I didn't kiss you."

"Of course. I understand." She didn't look at him.

"So you're okay about everything?" he pressed.

"As well as I can be. I'm not at all excited about facing everyone and telling them what we've done."

"You were perfectly willing to *pretend* we were married." He didn't understand why she was having a sudden attack of conscience. It seemed to him that it hadn't bothered her that much to intentionally mislead her family until now.

"Not because I want to deceive everyone. I just want my brothers to let me live my life the way I want. Is that too much to ask?"

"Hell, no, Lynn. I was pretty much doing the same thing until the night of Jake's wedding." Before he'd been trapped into this marriage fiasco.

His words caused her to look at him. "I didn't end up in your bed without your participation."

Russ's lips thinned. "Point taken."

"And I didn't mean for any of this to happen, you know. I was trying to save your job," she reminded him.

Russ took the turn off the main road. "Next time, let me defend myself." He was beginning to think that a beating by Ryder would have been less torture than being with Lynn all the time and not being able to touch her.

Hell, he was in for a ride. He hoped he was going to come out of this with his sanity intact.

"Don't worry, I will." His sarcastic tone annoyed

her. "You can start right now if you want to break the news," she suggested as they drove into the yard and he pulled the truck up to his quarters.

Taking the key from the ignition, he hesitated. "Uh, on second thought, why don't we wait until later."

Lynn caught herself smiling at him. "Biding time?"

"Hell, yes," Russ replied, and he grinned.

She gave him a relieved smile. "I'll tell them to expect you for dinner."

"Eloped?" Ashley jumped to her feet, and her chair scraped the floor as it was shoved back. Everyone at the dining room table stopped eating. Five pairs of eyes stared at Lynn and Russ.

Lynn blushed and looked from her sister-in-law to Russ, a smile frozen in place on her face. She hadn't expected her sister-in-law to be happy, and apparently she'd been right. They seemed to have taken them all by surprise. "Um, yes."

"Great!" Matthew grinned, obviously excited about the news of more family.

Ashley's head swivelled in his direction. "It is not *great,* Matthew! It means we missed seeing them get married, honey." She turned to face Lynn and Russ. "You really eloped? When?"

"This morning," Lynn confessed, then felt her face get even hotter. "We drove to San Luis." She stopped speaking for a moment. Their mystified expressions were almost funny. Almost. "We...we just decided not to wait." Russ was sitting next to her, and Lynn reached over and covered his hand with hers. "Right, sweetheart?"

Russ clasped her hand. "I tried to talk her into waiting, but she wouldn't listen."

Lynn gasped. "You did not!" She tried to yank her hand back, but he held on to it and wouldn't let go. Her eyes sent him a silent warning.

"Just kidding, honey," Russ said, and he grinned with a devilish glint in his eye.

"But what about the wedding we were planning?" Ashley wailed. Disappointment shadowed her eyes.

"Come here, darlin'," Ryder said, taking Ashley's hand. He scooted his seat back and tugged his pregnant wife down on his lap. "We should be happy for them. Besides, it's not the end of the world. Deke's still single. You can throw a wedding for him when he gets married."

"As if that'll happen," Jake quipped, then chuckled. He sobered when Ashley glared at him.

"I know we talked some about planning a wedding, but we really hadn't decided anything definite, yet," Lynn quickly reminded her. She looked apologetically at both Catherine and Ashley. "I, um, we appreciate all of the thought that you put into planning the wedding and that you wanted to make it really special, but we decided we wanted to be married right away."

"Oh, I wish you'd told us," Catherine said, her tone warm, but still disheartened. "We would've understood. Then we could've been there with you." She got up and walked around the table. Lynn stood to meet her and they hugged tightly. "I'm so happy for you."

Everyone got up from the table at that point, and Lynn and Russ accepted hugs and warm, heartfelt congratulations from them all. They all made their way into the den, except Matthew, who thought play-ing on his computer would be more interesting than listening to the adults discuss the event. Catherine and Ashley wanted to hear every detail of their wedding, and Lynn and Russ did their best to relate the events throughout the remainder of the evening.

Later, as the conversation quieted and it was near-ing time to go, Russ tackled the second hurdle of telling them that he and Lynn were moving off the Bar M. Feeling they wouldn't like it, he didn't look forward to seeing how Jake and Ryder were going to take the news.

He spoke to them all, but watched for Jake's re-action. "There's something else we need to tell you."

"You're pregnant!" Ashley blurted, looking at Lynn.

"No!" Both Russ and Lynn spoke at the same time. They looked at each other, then back at the group around the den.

"No, she's not pregnant," Russ said again firmly, and despite his best effort to prevent it, his tanned face darkened. It was the truth as far as he was con-cerned. He and Lynn really didn't know if she was.

"What is it then?" Catherine asked.

"We're moving." Russ didn't miss the fact that both Ryder and Jake turned their full attention to him.

"Moving where exactly?" Jake asked, and his words sounded close to a demand. He leaned forward in his chair, his facial muscles tightening. "When?"

"Russ bought the Peterson place. That's where we'll be living," Lynn told them.

Obviously pleased to hear his sister wasn't going far, Jake sat back, his shoulders relaxing. "The Pe-terson place? That meets our property line. I was interested in the land myself and wondered if they'd sold it when they moved."

"The timing was right, and Peterson and I made a deal before it went on the market," Russ explained.

"What are your plans?" Ryder asked.

"To start my own horse ranch. I hadn't planned on leaving the Bar M just yet, but—"

"Leaving?" Jake looked affronted at the idea.

"Well, not right away, but eventually, once I get some stock and get the ranch operational, I won't be staying on here."

"Hell, Russ," Jake interrupted. "I don't want to lose you, but stock isn't a problem." He nodded at Ryder. "We'll give you enough horses to get the ranch off the ground as a wedding gift."

Lynn was sitting in a chair, and Russ was perched on the arm of it beside her. His grip on her hand tightened as he shook his head. It was obvious to her that he wasn't comfortable with the idea.

"No, I—"

"We won't take no for an answer, will we, Ryder?"

"No way," her other brother agreed.

"You don't have to do this, Jake," Lynn said, aware of the tension in Russ.

"Lynn, you own a part of this ranch. Essentially, you'll be taking what belongs to you," Jake informed her in his usual compelling tone.

His words caused her chest to tighten. Had she jumped into this marriage to Russ prematurely? Would Jake have signed for the loan she'd wanted if she'd have asked?

Well, now she would never know, would she? For the time being, she and Russ were married, and there was nothing to do except make the best of it for a while until they could get out of it.

She looked at Russ, and his face was impassive. Jake spoke again and drew her attention.

"Russ, we'd like for you to continue putting in some time here for a while, if you think it's doable."

He nodded. "Sure. That'll work out fine. I'll continue to work here while getting things off the ground." Glancing up, he caught Lynn's eye. "You ready to leave?" he asked, hoping she was.

Lynn quickly got to her feet. "We'll be moving everything tomorrow. All help will be appreciated." She'd already packed a suitcase to take with her. Excusing herself, she went to get it. When she returned, Russ held his hand out to her as he took the suitcase from her.

"We'll see you tomorrow."

Everyone wished them well again, then they left and went across the yard to Russ's quarters. Russ had discreetly moved some of his things to his ranch, and although the Petersons had left a few pieces of furniture, they'd taken the beds. So that meant he and Lynn would be sharing the night in his room.

"That didn't go as bad as it could've," he commented, opening the door for her and waiting for her to go inside.

Lynn smiled brightly at him as she walked inside. "No it didn't. Oh my gosh, Russ," she said with excitement, spinning around to face him, "can you believe that we're gonna have horses? Our own horses?"

Russ censured her with a glare. "*You're* gonna have horses, sweetheart."

Looking offended, Lynn stared at him. "What?"

"They're gonna be your horses, not mine." He sat on a chair across from the bed.

"That's ridiculous. They're giving them to both of us."

"No, they're not," he said adamantly. "Essentially, as Jake pointed out, you own an interest in the Bar M. I'll help you train them, but don't think for a minute that I own any part of the horses you're getting." Marrying her had been the right thing to do, and he'd do it all over again to protect her. But he hadn't planned on Jake and Ryder giving them stock as a wedding gift.

It didn't really matter. He didn't consider them his. Lynn wasn't in love with him, and this marriage was a long ways from being real. She didn't want to stay married, and neither did he. Actually, when he thought about it, she was getting everything she'd wanted all along.

Lynn really didn't need him at all.

"Can we please not argue about this?" She clamped her lips together. Eyeing the rumpled bed as the only other place in the room to sit, she picked up her suitcase and started for the bathroom.

"Fine by me." Russ watched her walk into the bathroom and close the door. Seconds later, the shower came on. He didn't want to think about what she was doing, but he couldn't help it.

He wanted to be doing it *with* her.

Ten

Russ's gaze tracked Lynn's movements as she walked out of the bathroom and approached the bed. She'd put her clothes back on, and all he could think about was taking them off of her.

She moved to the bed and worked at straightening the covers. "I guess we're sharing, huh?" she asked, her expression hesitant.

"I guess." It was only one night. He could keep his hands off of her for one night, couldn't he? "Tomorrow, we'll be moved in at the ranch." If there had been a bed there, he'd have insisted that they spend the first night there instead of cooped up in his room together where she was close enough to smell, close enough to touch.

"Okay." She sat on the edge of the bed. "I guess I'll try to get some sleep."

Russ nodded and reached over and turned off one

of the lamps in the room. "Go ahead. I'll stay up a while," he said, leaving the one closest to him on. He wasn't sure what he was going to do, but he wasn't going to get in that bed with her. Not while he was hard and ready for her and she was so damn enticing.

She gave him a slight frown, then lowered herself to the bed on top of the covers. Turning her back to him, she settled her head on one of the pillows. Her butt wriggled as she tried to get comfortable, and Russ thought he'd go insane watching it.

He closed his eyes, wishing he had someplace else to go. But he knew it would look strange if he left, so he kept his rear in the chair. Slouching down, he crossed his arms over his chest and tried to get comfortable.

It was going to be one hell of a night.

Lynn woke in the morning and discovered she was alone in Russ's room. Her joints were stiff, and she stretched, trying to work out the soreness that she was sure she'd gotten from working on Russ's house. She was also aware that her stomach ached. Glancing at the clock, she saw that it was later than she usually slept. She hadn't eaten well the night before, so she probably just needed some breakfast.

Sitting up, she threw her feet to the floor, wondering where Russ was. Across the room, a pillow from the bed was on the chair. He must have spent the night there instead of sleeping beside her.

Despite her own stipulation that she and Russ wouldn't engage in sex, Lynn had been tortured with fantasies of him joining her during the night, taking her into his arms, and making love to her.

Well, obviously he wasn't that disturbed by keeping their relationship platonic because he hadn't once tried to cross that line. She was discovering that it was *she* who was having problems staying on her side of it.

What a way to spend your wedding night!

Sighing with pent-up frustration, she wondered where he was, what he'd been doing, how long he'd been gone? She got up, went into the bathroom and washed her face, then quickly changed her clothes. The last thing she needed was for one of her sisters-in-law to notice that she'd slept in them.

After pulling on her boots and jacket, she stepped outside and started for the house. She stopped dead in her tracks when she saw Russ's truck parked in front of it. It was loaded with some of the furniture from her bedroom!

Lynn covered the ground as fast as she could without running. As she started up the steps, Ashley and Catherine came out to meet her.

"What's going on?" she asked, and there was no way she could disguise the shock in her voice.

"We knew you were gonna have an...um," Ashley paused, glancing meaningfully at Catherine, "interesting night, so we thought we'd help you out by packing your things. We hope you don't mind." Her eyes were lit with excitement.

Catherine smiled at Lynn. "Russ, Ryder and Jake have already made one trip. They're inside getting the rest of your things. We were careful with everything, and we labeled all the boxes. All you have to do is unpack when you get home."

Lynn stared at them. It was obvious that both women thought that they'd been very helpful. She'd never intended to move everything she owned to Russ's ranch, only a little at a time, just enough to make it look real. Without causing suspicion, there was nothing Lynn could do but thank them.

"That was really, uh, nice of you." She looked around them and saw Russ and her brothers coming out of the house with boxes in their arms.

"Hey, darlin'," Ryder called, looking at Lynn. "We're just about to go over to Russ's room and put his furniture in the truck."

Lynn swallowed hard, and her gaze quickly found Russ's. He deposited a box in the truck, then promptly walked over to her.

"Morning, sweetheart." Without hesitation, he put his hand behind her neck, then his lips came down on hers.

His kiss shot fire through her veins, and she pressed closer to him. Before she had time to think, the kiss ended. He looked directly into her eyes. "Run ahead of us and get your things together," he said, and there was a warning in his eyes.

Lynn blinked, then went into motion, turning and hurrying across the yard. Damn! She didn't want her brothers to walk into Russ's room and discover that he'd spent the night in a chair!

Rushing inside, she threw the pillow from the chair onto the floor, then stripped the bed and tossed the covers on the floor with the pillow. She gathered her things and stuffed them in her suitcase. As she was closing it, the door opened and the men walked inside.

There was a discernable look of relief in Russ's eyes as he glanced around the room, and his gaze connected with Lynn's. She gave him a smile that looked sweet, but he knew her well enough to know that she felt the same way he did. Neither of them wanted her brothers to be suspicious of their marriage.

"All ready."

The men made quick work of moving the remainder of Russ's furniture to the truck. Ashley and Catherine had made Lynn promise to invite them over in a few days to see the place. Lynn drove her own truck behind Russ, and her brothers followed in Ryder's. By lunchtime, everything had been unloaded and placed in their new home, and Ryder and Jake had left.

Standing beside Russ in front of the house, Lynn watched her brothers drive away. "How on earth did all this happen?" she asked.

Russ chuckled. "I've got a better idea now of what you meant when you called Ashley and Catherine barracudas," he told her, and he couldn't help but laugh. "They got the idea that you'd want all of your things here right away, then put both of their husbands to work. I had to go along with it. I had no choice."

Lynn giggled. "I told you what they were like."

"Yeah, you did." He looked at the house, then at Lynn. Without thinking about what he was going to do, he swept her up in his arms.

"Russ!" She squealed and held on to his neck.

"Maybe this isn't like the real thing, but you deserve to be treated like a bride, so I'm gonna carry you inside."

The two-story farmhouse was old, but it had been well kept. The outside needed a little work, but had it really been her first home away from the Bar M, Lynn couldn't have been more happy with it.

"You don't have to do this," she told him, her tone husky.

"Yeah, I do," he answered, then proceeded to the door. He leaned down so Lynn could grab the handle of the screened door, then as she opened it, he shouldered it aside and crossed the threshold with her in his arms.

They stared at each other in silence, and electricity sparked between them. Russ's gaze dropped to her mouth. He'd known he was tempting himself by touching her, but he'd spent half the night watching her sleep in his bed. He couldn't take it any longer. He had to have a taste of her.

Just a taste, he promised himself.

He touched his mouth to hers, and she gasped, then made a sound of pleasure deep in her throat. Her hands, secured behind his neck, tightened. He deepened the kiss, touching her tongue with his.

Continuing to kiss her, Russ slowly lowered her legs to the floor, then slid his arms behind her back. Her hands rested on his chest, her palms flat against it and applying slight pressure.

Aware of her hesitation, Russ lifted his mouth from hers. "I'm sorry, I didn't mean for that to happen."

Lynn shook her head. "It's not that. I mean, I liked the kiss. I'm just not feeling too well. I didn't eat anything this morning, and my stomach feels upset."

Letting her go, Russ stepped away. "I don't think there's anything here to eat. Why don't we go into Crockett and get something? We can shop for groceries while we're there." He didn't want to go back to the Bar M. Crockett seemed safer, even if by now half the town would have heard rumors of their marriage.

"Okay. Let me just use the bathroom, and I'll be right back."

He watched her leave, then went into the kitchen. Hell, he was kidding himself. He wanted to make love to her. Right now and for as long as they were in this make-believe marriage. He wanted to satiate himself with her.

Maybe then he'd be able to come to terms with what it was going to feel like when the day came for them to part.

He was used to women leaving, wasn't he? Lynn wasn't any different. Sure, she was attracted to him, but her attraction didn't go beyond physical desire. He couldn't forget that. He wasn't going to do anything foolish, wasn't going to give her his trust.

Russ looked up when he heard Lynn walk into the room. Her face was colorless, her eyes teary. "You okay?"

She nodded, but it was obvious she wasn't. He approached her, but she stepped away from him. Frowning, he put his hand on his hip and studied her.

"What is it?"

Lynn felt as if her throat was clogged. Her hand went there and massaged it. "I'm not pregnant."

"You're not?" Russ sounded confused, then it dawned on him what she meant. "You mean you—"

"Yes," she answered, realizing now that her cramping stomach was her period starting, not hunger liked she'd assumed. Trying to keep her composure, she forced a laugh. "I guess the joke's on us, huh?" She didn't know what was wrong with her. She should have been feeling relieved, even happy, that she wasn't having Russ's baby. Instead, she had to fight the tears that threatened to expose her true emotions.

"Damn." Russ leaned against the kitchen counter. He didn't know what to say. She'd told him nerves and anxiety could cause her to be late, but he really hadn't believed it. He did feel relieved, he admitted silently. At least he wouldn't have to face her family and admit that he'd gotten her pregnant. He was also relieved that when he'd stated that she wasn't pregnant, he hadn't been lying.

"Yeah." Despite her best efforts, a tear escaped the corner of her eye. She nervously wiped it away as she watched for his reaction. It hurt to see that he was obviously relieved.

Disappointment filled her. She hadn't faced her true feelings, hadn't accepted that she was possibly falling in love with him. She realized now that all of her feelings toward Russ had been hidden. Having been overly concerned about being pregnant, she hadn't realized she was losing her heart.

Though she'd fought him on getting married, she'd actually been fighting her feelings for him. In fact, she'd gone ahead with the marriage because she was in love with him.

All of her hopes and dreams could have come true right here in this house with Russ, if he loved her.

But he didn't love her.

He'd married her because he'd thought she was pregnant, because he wanted to protect her reputation, because he didn't want to be the laughingstock of Crockett.

She could see all of that in his eyes.

He doesn't love you.

Lynn sniffed and wiped at the tears continuing to slide down her cheeks, hating that she was showing so much emotion in front of him. Gathering herself together, she looked at him. "We need to rethink our options."

His eyes darkened. "What do you mean?"

She gestured around them. "This is your home, not mine. I don't belong here, especially now. I'm thinking of coming clean to Jake and the rest of my family."

"Coming clean?" He straightened, but didn't move toward her.

"I think we should tell them everything. You know, that we'd never planned to marry at all, and that we're going to get an annulment."

"We're not telling anyone anything!" he ground out through clenched teeth. Furious, he stalked toward her. "Hell, your brothers would kill me. And the gossips in Crockett would be laughing at our expense. Maybe it wouldn't bother you, but I've been the butt of town jokes before, and I'm *not* gonna let it happen again. We're married, and we'll stay that way until all this dies down."

Russ felt like a fool. She'd only just learned that she wasn't pregnant, and she was ready to call an end to their arrangement. Well, he wasn't gonna let that happen.

Not yet.

"Well, exactly what do you want to do?" she demanded. "We can't just go on living together."

"We were going to do that anyway. Your not being pregnant doesn't change anything. Besides, we're not living together, we're *married*. I told you I was going

to marry you regardless. You were the one who didn't
accept that. It's done.''

"For how long?"

"As long as it takes."

"Meaning?"

"Hell, I don't know, Lynn. As long as necessary.''

"And you get to decide that?'' she argued, her tone
forceful. Was this how it was going to be? Russ making the decisions, controlling her life? It made her
want to scream.

"I'm not saying that, but we have to give it some
time. I've gone along with just about everything that
you've dragged me into. The least you can do is wait
for a while on this. What's it going to hurt?'' he demanded.

She shrugged, unable to come up with an argument
that made sense. "All right. We'll do it your way,''
she conceded grudgingly. "For a while.''

A week later, they'd just about settled into their
new home, though they were still waiting for their
phone to be hooked up. It had taken a few days to
unpack, but together they'd gotten all of the boxes
emptied and everything put away. Russ had insisted
on putting his bedroom furniture in one of the smaller
rooms because his bed was smaller than hers. Lynn
had argued with him, but she'd quit when he put her
bed together in the master bedroom.

They had just finished dinner when they heard a
vehicle pull up at the house, then someone laying on
the horn. By the time they both got out the door and
on the porch, Jake was out of his truck and running
to meet them.

"We need your help!'' he said in a rush, and his

tone was filled with concern. "Ashley's gone into labor."

Lynn stared at her brother with disbelief. "She's not due for another month!"

"I know. Ryder's really worried. Everything is probably fine, but I'm gonna fly them to San Antonio, just to be on the safe side. San Luis isn't equipped for any kind of prenatal emergencies."

"Are you ready to leave now?" Lynn asked.

He nodded. "Ryder's settling her in the plane, and I'd like to have Catherine come along with us, but that'll leave no one at home to watch the twins. Can you take care of them?"

"Of course." Lynn looked at Russ, and he agreed with a nod. "We'll come right over. We can stay at the ranch with them since all of their things are there."

"Great. I'm gonna head back then."

"What about Matthew?"

"He's coming along with us. He wants to be where the excitement is," Jake called over his shoulder, then hopped into his truck.

"We'll be right behind you," Russ called to him, fishing into his pocket for the key to his truck.

Lynn pulled the door to the house shut. By the time Jake had pulled away, she and Russ were in his truck following a short distance behind him. They arrived at the Bar M in record time. Catherine and Matthew handed over the babies to Lynn and Russ. Lynn gave Catherine instructions to call home as soon as they had news. She and Russ watched in silence as Jake drove the short distance to the landing strip.

Within minutes, the Cessna six-seater was in the air.

* * *

Lynn walked into the den, her hand on the back of her neck as she massaged her aching muscles. Russ was sitting on the sofa. He patted the seat next to him, and she dropped down on the soft leather and moaned. Her joints felt tense and stiff.

"I don't know how Ashley does it. If one of those babies even thinks of waking up before morning, I'm in trouble."

Russ grinned at her. "I know what you mean. They sort of suck the energy right out of you, don't they?"

She smiled to herself. "But they're so absolutely adorable that I don't really mind."

"Yeah." He watched as she rotated her shoulders. "Stiff?" She nodded, and Russ moved closer. "Turn around and I'll massage them for you."

Lynn obeyed immediately. She tilted her head down as his strong hands moved over her neck and shoulders, working out the tension in her muscles. "That feels so good." She moaned, and leaned back closer to him to give him better access.

"You've done a great job with the babies," Russ told her as he continued to soothe her aches. He admired her ability to take charge when she was needed, as well as the way she tenderly cared for the infants. It wasn't hard to see that she possessed natural tendencies for mothering. Though she hadn't wanted to be pregnant, and in fact they knew she wasn't, Russ was aware that she was going to be a great mother one day.

But not for your child.

The thought struck out of nowhere. It shouldn't have hurt, but it did. Though Russ had long ago decided that he'd never marry again and have children, he felt an unwelcome sense of anguish when he thought of Lynn getting on with her life after they separated.

"You've been a lot of help," she said, breaking into his thoughts. "I couldn't have handled those two without you." Russ had surprised her. He'd been attentive and cooperative, fetching what she needed, helping to feed the babies. During their baths, he'd handled the infants with gentle care. And earlier, when Melissa had fallen asleep in his arms, Lynn had felt a strong tug on her heart.

"I have to admit it's been an experience I'll never forget, but fun, too. Actually, they've been a lot easier to handle than I thought. They've hardly noticed that Ashley and Ryder aren't here."

"Thankfully everything went well with Ashley's delivery." They'd received a call the first night that Ashley had delivered a healthy baby boy, but since the infant came into the world under five pounds, the pediatrician tending him wanted to keep him a couple of extra days. That meant that Ashley would be staying also. Jake had asked Lynn if everything was okay at home. When she'd assured him they were fine and the babies were okay, he'd told Lynn that they'd all stay in San Antonio until the baby was released.

"I know Ryder's relieved. And with you taking care of the girls, he can focus his attention on Ashley and the new baby. What did they name him?"

Lynn turned her head toward him. Her gaze connected with his, and her heart suddenly stopped beating. His mouth was only inches from her own. "Um, what?" she asked, feeling a little disoriented.

Russ lost his train of thought, forgetting what he'd asked. His hands stilled on her shoulders as he gazed into her eyes. Her lips parted, and he could no longer fight his attraction to her. He'd kept his hands off of her like he'd promised, but it had been sheer hell in the interim.

He sucked in a hard breath as she turned her body more toward him and leaned closer. His mouth came down on hers as her hands started an exploration of their own, beginning by touching his face, then, as she twisted around to him, sliding down his neck and shoulders. He deepened the kiss, slipping his tongue past the barrier of her teeth, and she climbed into his lap to get closer to him.

Russ grunted as she straddled him, settling her rear against him, setting him on fire. Slipping his hand between them, he touched her breast, then felt the bud of her nipple as it became erect.

His breathing became hard as their passion escalated, and Russ combed his hands through her hair and cupped the back of her head as his tongue made a foray into her mouth. She whimpered, then pressed closer, her hips moving against his already burgeoning sex.

Russ lifted his mouth, trying hard to breathe and to keep his sense of reason. "I promised not to touch you," he rasped.

"I want you to touch me," Lynn whispered back, and her hands went to the buttons of his shirt.

He grabbed her wrists, holding them tight and stilling her movements. They stared at each other in stunned silence.

"Are you sure?" It cost him to ask, but he had to know that she really wanted this to happen between them, that she wouldn't be sorry later.

"Yes."

She followed up the simple answer by leaning forward and kissing his chin, then running her tongue along his cheek, planting more kisses on his skin as she made a path to his ear.

"Damn, Lynn, you're killing me."

She smiled, a cute little smile that made him want to take her right then and there. Instead, he scooted to the edge of the sofa and stood. Lynn squealed, then wrapped her legs around his waist.

"I want you naked and in bed. All night." Russ carried her through the house to Deke's room where she'd been sleeping. She continued to plant enticing kisses on his mouth until they reached the bed. He lowered her until her feet touched the floor, then they shed their clothes in a frenzied rush. They fell together in a tumble of arms and legs on the bed, and Russ moved over her, aligning their bodies.

He braced himself above her with his elbows, then touched his tongue to her breast, kissing it, then sucking the nipple into his mouth as he carcssed her other breast with his hand.

Lynn's hips moved rhythmically as his hand slipped between her legs, and he touched her intimately. She was hot and wet, ready for him, and his erection grew harder. He was poised and ready to enter her when he stopped.

"Hold on," he whispered, then stretched across the bed to the floor where he'd dropped his pants. He yanked out his wallet and flipped it open. In his hurried movements to get the one condom he had tucked in it, the contents spilled onto the floor. After a moment, Russ returned to her, settling himself between her legs.

Ready for him, Lynn locked her legs around him as he came into her, her back arching as his hands slid beneath her buttocks. He plunged harder, deeper. Her hands moved across his back, then her fingers tightened, pinching his skin as she cried out with pleasure. He climaxed only moments later, falling into a dark void.

Eleven

———

Russ came awake slowly. He rolled to his side and reached for Lynn, then opened his eyes when he realized she wasn't there. He shouldn't have been surprised, he guessed, to discover he was in bed alone.

But, dammit, he was.

Surprised and disappointed.

Was it because Lynn already regretted what had happened between them last night? Or was she merely going through the ritual of getting the babies up and dressed for the day?

He'd rather believe the latter, but doubts plagued him. Surely by now she realized the same thing he did...during the night they'd had unprotected sex, which basically put them right back where they'd started. Swearing under his breath, he climbed out of the bed. He quickly located his jeans and underwear and slid them on, then reached for his shirt.

He went in search of Lynn and found her and the babies in the kitchen. He stood silently at the door and watched her as she moved about the room. She was good with the girls. She'd seen to their every need, automatically knowing what to do for each of them as if they were her own. He could easily see her mothering her own child.

His child.

Russ silently cursed, telling himself he was a fool if he let down his guard around Lynn. Sure she enjoyed his lovemaking, but that was all there was between them. And that's the way he wanted it to be, wasn't it? It was the only way he knew to protect his heart. He'd trusted his heart to a woman before, and had been hurt by her betrayal. He wasn't going to give Lynn that kind of power over him.

He should have learned his lesson the hard way, but it seemed his desire for Lynn had taken over his common sense, and he was constantly having to refocus. They made love several times during the night. He'd protected Lynn the first time with the only condom he'd had. He'd convinced himself that he could be satisfied with making love to her only once. And dammit, he probably would have if she hadn't curled against his body afterward.

Holding her against him had been his undoing. Before they'd fallen asleep, they'd begun touching, which led to kissing, which led to him burying himself inside her so fast that they'd both climaxed within moments. It had felt natural and right, and sex with Lynn had satisfied him beyond his imagination.

The third time, he awakened with her sprawled all over him and any sense of responsibility had been nonexistent. Never in his life had he felt so overwhelmed with emotion, so deep a desire for a woman that he couldn't think straight.

Not just any woman.

Just Lynn.

Hell.

He quietly walked up to her and stood behind her, then touched her shoulders. She squealed, then dropped the knife in her hand and spun around.

"Russ!"

"Who'd you think it was?" he teased, loving the soft pink flush that rose to her cheeks. He bent to kiss her, and she raised herself on the tip of her toes to meet him. Russ slid his arms around her back and held her against him.

"I just didn't hear you," Lynn whispered, and her heart skipped a beat. She hadn't expected him to be so open with affection. It both surprised and pleased her. "I'm about ready to feed the girls," she said. "Wanna help?"

"Sure." Russ reached around her for a piece of pancake that she hadn't yet cut into tiny bite-size pieces and popped it into his mouth.

"I made coffee if you want some." She pointed to the other end of the counter. Russ didn't let her go, and she cocked her head and looked at him. "You know, those two aren't going to wait much longer," she pointed out, nodding toward the twins secured in high chairs near the table.

"Yeah, I know." Reluctantly, Russ released her and walked over to pour himself a cup of hot coffee.

Lynn traced his movements with her gaze as she put two small plates of pancake pieces in front of the girls, then turned her attention to them. Each baby squealed in their own special way as they grabbed bites of pancake and stuffed them in their mouths. She glanced back at Russ, who was stirring sugar into his cup.

She was glad he hadn't brought up their night of lovemaking and how it had compromised their situation. Up an hour ahead of him, she'd checked on the babies and had found them still sleeping. Hurrying, she'd had just enough time to shower and change before she'd heard them awaken. By the time she'd gotten to their room, they were both wide awake and itching to get up. While changing them, she'd tried to analyze her feelings. She'd come up with every rationalization imaginable, and finally she'd admitted the truth to herself.

She'd fallen in love with Russ.

Hopelessly, desperately in love with him.

She wasn't sure he would be all that happy about it if she admitted it to him. Sure, he was attracted to her, but she also knew he felt trapped into this situation by circumstances over which he had no control. If he'd had the opportunity to choose this path, she knew in her heart that he wouldn't have chosen to be with her.

He still insisted that they should stay married long enough to stop the townsfolk from gossiping and after a reasonable amount of time, they could get an annulment.

Divorce.

Lynn swallowed hard as an unexpected ache centered in her chest. A annulment was no longer an option, was it? They would have to get a divorce. Her heart wanted to believe that maybe Russ could love her, that maybe she could be the woman to claim his heart.

Maybe if they spent this time together living as man and wife, he would *want* to stay married. It was possible, right?

She vowed to enjoy the next couple of days with him and see where it would lead. If a broken heart was in her future, she'd deal with that when it came around. She was going to seize this opportunity to be with Russ, to enjoy loving him, and maybe, just maybe, he'd fall in love with her, too.

As Lynn had hoped, the next two days went by with her and Russ enjoying each other's company. They played with the twins, who seemed to be energy-filled little humans. Russ had been busy, leaving for a few hours to see to things at their ranch because they'd already started housing the horses that Jake and Ryder had given them. He'd also checked on the men taking care of the Bar M, seeing to its smooth operation, then returned by dinnertime. By the time Michelle and Melissa were in bed for the evening, Lynn and Russ were more than ready for some time alone.

Russ hadn't said a word about their lack of birth control the first night they'd been together, but he'd been sure to let her know that he'd picked up some protection. Lynn had nodded and smiled, then welcomed him into her arms. Their time alone was spent mostly in bed. After putting the babies to bed, they'd only left Deke's room for food. They'd grabbed snacks and fed each other as they watched a little television, then inevitably they'd start kissing and touching and end up making love.

Unfortunately their time together came to an abrupt end when they got a phone call from Jake. He reported that Ashley and the baby were being released from the hospital, and they would be arriving home before dusk. Lynn tidied the house, and she and Russ tended to the babies and had them fed and bathed by the time their parents got there.

The newest McCall was welcomed with wide, inquisitive eyes by his older sisters. Michelle and Melissa, though curious about the tiny infant, actually seemed more interested in vying for Ashley and Ryder's attention. Unlike his sisters, the baby, named Taylor Mitchell, had the McCall blond hair and the same blue eyes as his father.

Lynn and Russ had cooked dinner for everyone, and for a while they sat around the table to discuss the details of the infant's birth. Ryder quickly reported that he'd made it through Taylor's entire birth process without fainting, as if he'd thought that it would help him live down the fact that he'd passed out in the delivery room when the twins were born. Lynn and Russ also got a thorough briefing on the neonatal care the tiny infant had received at the hospital. Once everything had settled down and their services were no longer needed, Lynn and Russ decided to leave and go home.

Yet, as they walked back into their own house, a strange and unwelcome tension filled the air between them. While they had talked and teased and entertained each other during their stay at the McCall ranch, they said little as they returned to their real world.

The reminder that they'd slept in separate bedrooms only days ago was blatant evidence of their true relationship. Lynn had decided not to make an issue of it, hoping that they'd become more comfortable around each other as the evening progressed.

Russ, however, felt altogether differently. He was sure that nothing between them had changed except that they'd made love. Lynn was still the same woman who had wanted her freedom only days ago. Though he wanted her to share his bed, he realized that he had no right to expect her to. Sure he could seduce her and make love to her, and they could play at being happy together for a while, but eventually she'd blame him for holding her back, for stealing her dreams.

He couldn't do that to her, or to himself. He wasn't the man for her, couldn't give her the love and devotion that she deserved. It was his pride that kept her locked into their marriage. He'd have to swallow it and let her go.

Also, he was cognizant of the fact that they hadn't discussed the possibility of her being pregnant either. It was an issue that lay before them, and whether they wanted to face it or not, it had to be discussed.

He started to confront her, but stopped when she looked at him, her blue eyes questioning. "I'll go check on the horses," he said, stalling for time.

"Sure." She didn't offer to go with him.

Nodding, he turned and walked out the back door. Lynn watched him leave, and her heart sank. They'd crossed a line in their relationship, one it seemed Russ had no trouble ignoring during the past few days when he'd made love to her but apparently felt he must adhere to now that they were alone.

She waited for a while for him to return, wanting so much to talk to him. But it soon became apparent to her that he wasn't coming in. Finally, she gave up and went to bed, hoping that he'd join her, but knowing in her heart that he wasn't going to.

Three weeks went by and most of those hours they spent apart. Russ left early to see to the business of running the McCall ranch, then returned later in the day to help with chores at home. Lynn spent the mornings feeding the horses and raking out their stalls, then turned to the business of training. While once just being around them gave her such joy, the horses were now a reminder of what they were going to eventually cost her.

Her heart.

She and Russ were sharing a house, but it wasn't a home. They were raising horses, training them, but Russ didn't consider them his. She loved her new home, but it didn't belong to her. Everything she ever wanted was now within her grasp, except her heart's desire—Russ's love.

He had called earlier and told her he'd be late getting back due to a sick animal at the Bar M. Keeping his dinner warm, she waited hours for him to return, wanting to talk, to get it all out in the open. She heard his truck pull up to the house, and her heart lurched. She'd half expected him to remain distant as he'd been over the past few weeks.

Instead, he stepped into the kitchen and walked over to the sink. He scrubbed his hands, then taking a towel from a rack on the wall, he dried them, then tossed the towel aside as he turned to look at her.

"We need to talk, Lynn."

Lynn started. Though she'd wanted to talk, his tone sent icy shivers down her spine. She didn't want to hear what he had to say, yet there was no turning back. It was time for her to face the inevitable.

He either loved her or he didn't.

She drew a deep breath and looked at him. His face

was unreadable, and it was as if the man she'd made love with no longer existed. "All right."

His lips thinned. "I know you could be pregnant. I should have protected you," he stated bluntly, not beating around the bush.

"It's just as much my fault." She didn't want him to blame himself. "I'm just as responsible."

Russ glared at her, his frustration mounting. "You said before that you could tell if you were pregnant from a pregnancy test."

She nodded. "Yes."

"I think we should get one as soon as possible." Though he'd told her that he wanted to stay married to her until the town had no reason to gossip about them, he knew it wasn't possible. His pride be damned, he couldn't go on living with her without touching her.

"Sure. I'll get one," she told him, and her tone was sharper than she'd intended. "Catherine asked me to go to San Luis with her to pick up some things that Ashley needs. I'll slip away and get a test while I'm there."

"All right." That decided, Russ moved away from the counter, then stopped in front of her. "If you're not pregnant, I'll give you what you want. I won't keep you here any longer."

"What?" Lynn's heart twisted with pain.

"You never wanted any of this," he stated roughly, "and neither did I. I trapped you into it, trapped us both into it. I know I insisted on staying together, but that was my pride talking," he admitted candidly.

He doesn't love you.

The stabbing pain in Lynn's heart grew sharper, stealing her ability to breathe. "But I thought—"

"What? That we'd try to make something more of this?" He waved his hand in the air, then rubbed the back of his neck. "I'm not what you want, Lynn," he said, trying to make her face the truth. "Sure, we're great in bed together, but that doesn't change anything."

"Yes, but—"

"Before all this happened, you wanted your freedom. You wanted to have your own ranch, to raise and train horses. Have you changed your mind?"

"No." She still wanted those things, but she wanted Russ's love more.

He nodded. "I'm giving you the ranch."

His words stunned her. She put her hand against the table to check her balance. "I'm not going to take your ranch, Russ. That's ridiculous!"

"It isn't when you reason it out. This is what you've wanted all along. You never set out to end up married to a ranch hand. The truth is, I never intended to ever get married again. You know that." He shrugged his big shoulders. "I won't be hanging around anyway. I think it's time for me to move on."

Because of her. She swallowed hard, trying to dislodge the knot in her throat. He'd told her that he'd never intended to get married again. Why had she thought that being intimate with her had changed anything?

"Is that what you really want? To be free to leave?"

"Freedom is what we both wanted," he reminded her, his gaze unwavering.

"Then I'll get the test," she said in a barely audible tone.

Russ stared at her a moment longer. Without saying

anything more, he turned and left the kitchen. Lynn
felt the room close in on her. She sank into a chair,
leaned forward and held her head in her hands.

He doesn't love you.

She had to face the truth, no matter how hard it
was, no matter how very much it hurt. He did care
for her. He wouldn't be making the sacrifice of giving
her the ranch if he didn't. But he didn't love her, and
that's what she wanted from him.

His love.

The next day, Lynn returned from San Luis with a
pregnancy test. It hadn't been easy for her to get away
from Catherine, but she'd managed it. She'd pur-
posely carried along a large handbag so she could
tuck the test in it and Catherine would never know.

Lynn waved at Catherine as she drove away, then
turned and walked into the house. Russ was nowhere
around, and she figured he was over at the Bar M.

Relieved, she pulled the pregnancy kit from her bag
and went into the main bathroom, her heart hammering. Moments later, a little blue dot told her the re-
sults.

She was pregnant.

You're carrying Russ's baby.

The confirmation of her pregnancy caused her legs
to go weak. She slipped to the bathroom floor in a
heap and began to cry as the pregnancy stick fell to
the floor. What was she going to do now? Russ didn't
love her. He'd already made that clear.

But he was a man bound by duty. He'd proved that
by marrying her when he thought her reputation as
well as his was fodder for gossip, when there was a
chance before that she was pregnant.

He doesn't love you.

But he would insist on staying married, wouldn't he, if he knew she was pregnant? Wracked by the emotions raging inside her, Lynn sobbed. She didn't want Russ to stay married to her out of obligation. If he didn't love her, she'd eventually learn to live with it, but there was no way she'd hold him in a marriage he didn't want.

Lynn cried until no more tears came. When she finally quieted, she forced herself to get up and wash her face, then she drew in a deep breath. She could get through this. She quickly gathered the items from the test and stuffed them into the box, then threw it in the wastebasket. All she had to do was tell Russ that the test was negative. He would never know otherwise.

He would walk out of her life and never know that they'd created a child together.

When Russ came in late that evening, the kitchen was dark. He flipped on the light switch, and his gaze fell on the slim form sitting in one of the chairs at the table. Regarding Lynn, he wondered why she'd been sitting there in the dark.

"Is something wrong?"

She shook her head. "No. Actually, everything is fine." She struggled to maintain her composure, and it took every ounce of strength and courage for her to forge ahead. "I did the pregnancy test today. We got lucky. I'm not pregnant."

"You're not?" As he spoke, the coiled tension inside him vanished, and his shoulders sagged. "You're sure?"

"Yes," she said a little too brightly.

His mouth tightened a fraction as he nodded. "Then I'll be leaving by the end of the week." He turned away.

"Russ—" Lynn called out to him.

He stopped, then swivelled around and looked at her.

"You don't have to go. I can move back to the Bar M."

"There's no reason for you to do that. I'm leaving anyway, and this place is big enough for you to raise as many horses as you want. You might as well stay here as look for someplace else. It's close to the Bar M, and I know Jake and Ryder would like to have you nearby."

He walked out without saying anything more. Lynn went to her room to get her keys to her truck. She had to get out of there before she fell apart. She didn't know where she'd go, but she couldn't stay in the house with Russ another moment.

Tears blurred her eyes as she looked around her. She swiped at her face, brushing them away. Then she spotted the keys on the floor where they'd apparently fallen earlier. Snatching them up, she started from the room, but stopped short when Russ was suddenly standing in front of her, blocking her path.

"I'm going out for a while."

She started to move around him, but he stepped in front of her again, blocking her from leaving. "Not so fast." Taking her by the arm, he dragged her back into her bedroom. "What's this?" he demanded, letting her go.

Lynn's eyes widened, and she stared at the pregnancy stick in his hand. She backed away a step. "What?"

Russ's gut twisted. "I found it on the bathroom floor, then I saw the box in the trash. You lied, didn't you?" Fury blinded him, making him unable to focus on anything but the fact that she'd kept the truth from him.

She shook her head, and he snorted. "Dammit, tell me the truth, Lynn." He waved the stick in front of her face. "You're pregnant with my baby, aren't you?"

Lynn stared back at him, then increased the distance between them. She'd never seen Russ so angry. "All right, yes. I'm pregnant," she admitted, a guilty blush rising to her cheeks. "But I didn't lie about the baby to hurt you."

"Now why don't I believe that?" His eyes bore into her, his face twisting with anger. "You had me fooled, honey." He visibly shook. Pain seared him, and he advanced on her. He'd thought he'd kept her at a distance. He hadn't thought she could hurt him. But she had.

Just like every other woman in your past.

"I thought I was doing what was best for both of us," she insisted, defending her actions.

"By not telling me about the baby?"

"You said you didn't want to be married! I knew if you found out I was pregnant, that you'd insist that we stayed together."

"And that's not what you wanted, is it?" he asked harshly. "You just figured you'd lie, then stay here on the ranch and get that freedom that's so damned important to you." His tone was bitter.

"No—"

"Don't lie to me again, do you understand?"

"I'm sorry," Lynn whispered shakily. "I didn't mean to hurt you, Russ."

"Yeah, right," he said severely. "You acted like you didn't want this ranch, too, but that's what you wanted all along, isn't it?"

She paled. "I wanted a ranch, yes, but not yours."

"I don't believe you."

"But you have to. I know you think this is what I want, but it isn't." His expression remained hard as stone. "Listen to me," she pleaded, wanting to make him understand that she hadn't meant to hurt him. "I do want to raise horses, but I never wanted to take the ranch from you. I didn't lie to you to hurt you, I swear."

He stared at her, his green gaze piercing. "Why did you lie, then, Lynn? Why couldn't you have told me the truth?"

"Because...because I love you!" she told him, blurting out the truth.

Russ whitened, then recovered his composure. "Yeah, right." He wasn't about to believe that one. He was gullible when it came to Lynn, even stupid sometimes. But there was no way he was going to swallow her desperate attempt to smooth things over.

"It's the truth, Russ. I do love you." She started to touch him, but his cold gaze froze her movements. "Okay, I'll admit I didn't want to fall in love with you. I thought I wanted my freedom. It was so important to me to be able to think for myself, to choose my own path in life. When we made love after Jake's wedding, I knew I was in trouble. I started thinking about you all the time, and that's why I was so determined to end what was happening between us. You were a threat to all I thought I wanted. I wouldn't let myself believe that I was falling in love with you."

He grimaced. "And, you want me to believe that your freedom isn't important anymore?"

"Not if it means losing you, Russ. It's because I value the right to make my own choices that I didn't tell you about the baby," she insisted. Testing him, she moved closer. "I love you. I thought you wanted to leave, and I was letting you go because that's what *you* wanted." She reached toward him, and despite the way he flinched, she placed her hand on his chest.

"How can I believe you?" he asked, holding himself back from touching when that's what he wanted to do more than anything in the world. He wanted to gather her in his arms and hold her and never let her go.

His heart was pounding. She could feel it beneath her palm. "Listen to your heart, Russ. What happened between us was meant to happen because we belong together."

Russ drew in a deep breath. He wanted to believe her, but the women in his life had taught him differently. Lynn moved closer, and she put her hands on his cheeks, forcing him to look at her.

"I don't want you to go. I want you to stay here and love me back."

She was going to let you go because she thought that was what you wanted.

Russ's heart began to melt. As he watched her, her beautiful blue eyes teared, and he realized she was telling him the truth. Her love had been there all along, but he hadn't been able to see past his anger. She'd been willing to let him go, even though she was carrying his child, a tie that could bind them together. She was ready to face her family and tell them about her pregnancy without him there to support her. Lynn had been willing to give him the very thing that she held sacred.

Freedom.

"Come here." Gently grabbing her by the arms, he pulled her against him. "I'm never going to let you go, you know that?" he asked, his voice slightly rough.

She slid her arms around his back. "Do you promise?"

Russ's mouth came down hard on hers, and he kissed her deeply. Then he lifted his head and gazed into her eyes. "I promise with all my heart."

She hesitated, lowering her gaze for a moment before looking back up at him. Her heart wanted to believe him, but she needed to be reassured. "But you were leaving."

"I knew how much you wanted to be on your own. That's why I was leaving—to give you what you said you wanted."

She kissed his mouth, then searched his face. "I don't want to be free of you, Russ. I want to stay married to you."

"I want that, too."

"Are you sure?" He hadn't said he loved her, nor had he said what he thought about her being pregnant. "How do you feel about the baby?" she asked quietly. Was there room in his heart for his child?

"I'm gonna love our baby, Lynn. I never had a mother and father to raise me, and I've always wanted the things I'd been denied all my life. I've lived alone a long time, and I'd resigned myself to never having children. Honey, I want our baby. I want to be right here with you raising it." He stopped speaking and stared at her.

"I want that, too, Russ, but there's something I want even more." Her eyes watered again, and a tear slid down her cheek. "I want your love."

Russ's lips turned upward. "I'm going to love you for the rest of your life, Lynn. I told you once that I don't lie. I'm not lying now. I love you—so much that I ache with it. I think I knew it all along inside my heart, but my mind just wouldn't let go of the hurt and pain of my past."

"I'm sorry—"

"Don't feel sorry for me, honey," he whispered fiercely. "Your love is enough to make me happy for the rest of my life. Believe me, sweetheart, I'd marry you all over again if you wanted me to."

She grinned at him then, her eyes lighting with joy. "I think I know another way that you can convince me." Her eyes twinkled merrily.

Russ looked at her with caution. He loved her desperately. He'd do anything for her. "Yeah?"

She kissed him, molding her mouth to his. Russ groaned when her tongue touched his, then retreated as she lifted her lips. "Come on, cowboy," she said, smiling. She took his hand and drew him toward the bed. "Prove it."

Russ had to hand it to her. She knew just the way he could prove how much he loved her.

And he did.

* * * * *

Silhouette® Desire.

presents

DYNASTIES: THE CONNELLYS

A brand-new miniseries about the Connellys of Chicago, a wealthy, powerful American family tied by blood to the royal family of the island kingdom of Altaria. They're wealthy, powerful and rocked by scandal, betrayal…and passion!

Look for a whole year of glamorous and utterly romantic tales in 2002:

January: **TALL, DARK & ROYAL by Leanne Banks**
February: **MATERNALLY YOURS by Kathie DeNosky**
March: **THE SHEIKH TAKES A BRIDE by Caroline Cross**
April: **THE SEAL'S SURRENDER by Maureen Child**
May: **PLAIN JANE & DOCTOR DAD by Kate Little**
June: **AND THE WINNER GETS…MARRIED! by Metsy Hingle**
July: **THE ROYAL & THE RUNAWAY BRIDE by Kathryn Jensen**
August: **HIS E-MAIL ORDER WIFE by Kristi Gold**
September: **THE SECRET BABY BOND by Cindy Gerard**
October: **CINDERELLA'S CONVENIENT HUSBAND by Katherine Garbera**
November: **EXPECTING…AND IN DANGER by Eileen Wilks**
December: **CHEROKEE MARRIAGE DARE by Sheri WhiteFeather**

Silhouette®
Where love comes alive™

Visit Silhouette at www.eHarlequin.com

SDDYN02

eHARLEQUIN.com

community | membership

buy books | authors | online reads | magazine | learn to write

buy books

Your one-stop shop for great reads at great prices. We have all your favorite Harlequin, Silhouette, MIRA and Steeple Hill books, as well as a host of other bestsellers in Other Romances. Discover a wide array of new releases, bargains and hard-to-find books today!

learn to write

Become the writer you always knew you could be: get tips and tools on how to craft the perfect romance novel and have your work critiqued by professional experts in romance fiction. Follow your dream now!

Silhouette®

Where love comes alive™—online...

Visit us at
www.eHarlequin.com

SINTLTW

ANN MAJOR
CHRISTINE RIMMER
BEVERLY BARTON

cordially invite you to attend the year's most exclusive party at the **LONE STAR COUNTRY CLUB!**

Meet three very different young women who'll discover that wishes *can* come true!

LONE STAR COUNTRY CLUB:
The Debutantes

Lone Star Country Club: Where Texas society reigns supreme—and appearances are *everything*.

Available in May at your favorite retail outlet, only from Silhouette.

Silhouette ®
Where love comes alive ™

Visit Silhouette at www.eHarlequin.com   PSLSCCTD

Silhouette Books presents a dazzling keepsake
collection featuring two full-length novels by
international bestselling author

DIANA PALMER

Brides To Be

(On sale May 2002)

THE AUSTRALIAN
*Will rugged outback rancher Jonathan Sterling
be roped into marriage?*

HEART OF ICE
*Close proximity sparks a breathtaking attraction between a
feisty young woman and a hardheaded bachelor!*

You'll be swept off your feet by Diana Palmer's BRIDES TO BE.

Don't miss out on this special two-in-one volume, available soon.

*Available only from Silhouette Books
at your favorite retail outlet.*

Silhouette®

Where love comes alive™

Visit Silhouette at www.eHarlequin.com   PSBTB

You are invited to enter the exclusive, masculine world of the...

Silhouette Desire's powerful miniseries features five wealthy Texas bachelors—all members of the state's most prestigious club—who set out to uncover a traitor in their midst... and discover their true loves!

THE MILLIONAIRE'S PREGNANT BRIDE
by Dixie Browning
February 2002 (SD #1420)

HER LONE STAR PROTECTOR
by Peggy Moreland
March 2002 (SD #1426)

TALL, DARK...AND FRAMED?
by Cathleen Galitz
April 2002 (SD #1433)

THE PLAYBOY MEETS HIS MATCH
by Sara Orwig
May 2002 (SD #1438)

THE BACHELOR TAKES A WIFE
by Jackie Merritt
June 2002 (SD #1444)

Available at your favorite retail outlet.

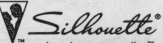

Where love comes alive™

Visit Silhouette at www.eHarlequin.com   SDTCC02

If you enjoyed what you just read,
then we've got an offer you can't resist!

Take 2 bestselling
love stories FREE!
Plus get a FREE surprise gift!

Clip this page and mail it to Silhouette Reader Service™

IN U.S.A.
3010 Walden Ave.
P.O. Box 1867
Buffalo, N.Y. 14240-1867

IN CANADA
P.O. Box 609
Fort Erie, Ontario
L2A 5X3

YES! Please send me 2 free Silhouette Desire® novels and my free surprise gift. After receiving them, if I don't wish to receive anymore, I can return the shipping statement marked cancel. If I don't cancel, I will receive 6 brand-new novels every month, before they're available in stores! In the U.S.A., bill me at the bargain price of $3.34 plus 25¢ shipping and handling per book and applicable sales tax, if any*. In Canada, bill me at the bargain price of $3.74 plus 25¢ shipping and handling per book and applicable taxes**. That's the complete price and a savings of at least 10% off the cover prices—what a great deal! I understand that accepting the 2 free books and gift places me under no obligation ever to buy any books. I can always return a shipment and cancel at any time. Even if I never buy another book from Silhouette, the 2 free books and gift are mine to keep forever.

225 SEN DFNS
326 SEN DFNT

Name _____ (PLEASE PRINT)

Address _____ Apt.# _____

City _____ State/Prov. _____ Zip/Postal Code _____

* Terms and prices subject to change without notice. Sales tax applicable in N.Y.
** Canadian residents will be charged applicable provincial taxes and GST.
All orders subject to approval. Offer limited to one per household and not valid to current Silhouette Desire® subscribers.
® are registered trademarks of Harlequin Enterprises Limited.

DES01   ©1998 Harlequin Enterprises Limited

In April 2002,

Silhouette®

Desire

presents a sizzling new
installment in the
wildly popular

LONG, TALL
Texans

miniseries from
beloved author

DIANA PALMER

A MAN OF MEANS (SD #1429)

From the moment powerfully seductive
Rey Hart first set eyes on Meredith Johns,
he became mesmerized by the lovely
young woman. For not only did Meredith
stir the hot-tempered cattleman's soul with
her gentle innocence, he discovered she
was a top-notch biscuit maker! However,
installing Meredith on the Hart ranch as
Rey's coveted cook was a cinch compared
to breaking the potent spell she had cast
over his heavily armored heart....

Don't miss this long-awaited
Long, Tall Texans tale from international
bestselling author Diana Palmer!

Available at your favorite retail outlet.

Silhouette®

Where love comes alive™

Visit Silhouette at www.eHarlequin.com   SDMAN